PURRFECT MODEL

THE MYSTERIES OF MAX 52

NIC SAINT

PURRFECT MODEL

The Mysteries of Max 52

Copyright © 2022 by Nic Saint

All rights reserved. No part of this book may be reproduced in any form by any electronic or mechanical means including photocopying, recording, or information storage and retrieval without permission in writing from the author.

This is a work of fiction. Names, characters, places, brands, media, and incidents are either the product of the author's imagination or are used fictitiously. The author acknowledges the trademarked status and trademark owners of various products referenced in this work of fiction, which have been used without permission. The publication/use of these trademarks is not authorized, associated with, or sponsored by the trademark owners.

Edited by Chereese Graves

www.nicsaint.com

Give feedback on the book at: info@nicsaint.com

facebook.com/nicsaintauthor
@nicsaintauthor

First Edition

Printed in the U.S.A

PURRFECT MODEL

Anyone Can Paint

When Jay met Laia, it was love at first sight. But when Laia's parents met Jay, disaster struck. To such an extent they forced her to choose between her family and her fiancé. Laia chose her fiancé, and that's when the trouble started. The young couple soon became the victims of a harassment campaign, which led them to Odelia, who promised she would find the vicious stalker intent on their destruction.

And then of course there was the whole art class fiasco. I'd tell you more, but sometimes it's best to find out for oneself. Also, I still haven't fully recovered. Let's just say that a sudden wave of artistic fervor swept across our family, affecting first Marge and Harriet, then Gran, then Tex, and finally even Grace, the most recent addition to the family roster. Suffice it to say, things soon turned ugly. Very ugly.

CHAPTER 1

It should have been the happiest day of Laia's young life. The day she was to introduce her future husband to her parental unit. And it probably would have been the day that all the world waited with bated breath to see who Mr. Lucky was, if it hadn't been for one small snag: the response of Mr. and Mrs. Twine, which wasn't as ecstatic as it could have been. In actual fact, it was anything but.

And it had all started so well. She'd phoned Mommy and told her she had a nice surprise in store. She should have known not everything was as it should have been, for Mommy's response had been remarkably lacking in the kind of warm excitement a future bride likes to see. But she'd ignored it and had ascribed it to Mommy being in a bad mood, as tended to happen more often lately.

Jay must have realized something was amiss, for he'd immediately said, "Maybe we should postpone, my blossom."

"No, we're doing this now," she had told him. They'd waited long enough, in her estimation. They had, after all, been engaged for all of two weeks, and had known each other exactly three months, which meant something. She'd never been with one guy for longer than a couple of weeks before, so three months told her that Jay was for keeps, and was to be the man next to whom she wanted to wake up for the rest of her life. The man whose face she would see looking back at her across the breakfast table, asking her to pass the maple syrup and strawberry jam. Like Mommy and Daddy, who'd been happily married now for twenty-five years.

It was the kind of eternal bond she had always envisioned for herself. The kind of marital bliss she'd always known would someday be in the cards for her as well.

On the drive over, Jay remarked, "Maybe you shouldn't tell them we're engaged. Maybe introduce me as a good friend instead. Then we can gradually work our way up to being boyfriend and girlfriend, and eventually spring the marriage thing on them."

"Oh, don't be silly," she said as she steered the car along the familiar route. "My parents are modern people. They have always raised me to be independent and follow my own path. I'm sure they'll be thrilled to hear I'm getting married."

"If you say so," her fiancé murmured, clearly not entirely convinced.

The little car hurtled along the road, and she wondered if her parents would buy her a new car now that she had reached this milestone in a young girl's life. Or maybe even a new apartment?

They still thought that she was living in her own flat, for which they paid rent, but the truth was that she had given up the flat and had moved in with Jay, pocketing the rent herself and spending it on some necessary repairs that had made Jay's loft more suitable for a young couple in love. Minor things like a working gas heater and decent plumbing. And of course mending that hole in the roof. The incessant cooing of a family of pigeons who had come to regard part of the loft as their personal home had been a romantic notion at first, but not so much when it rained and she'd woken up from a cold shower one morning.

Jay was an artist, of course, and artists don't care about such minor practical inconveniences, focusing on their art first and foremost, and probably not even noticing things like a leaky roof. But Laia, who'd grown up in outrageous riches, had found the sudden descent into the bohemian life jarring to say the least.

It was one of the reasons she'd decided to come clean, and admit that she was to become Mrs. Jay Green very soon now. She wanted to return to the kind of lifestyle to which she'd grown accustomed, and even though she knew in her heart of hearts that it was only a matter of time before Jay would become a star and money would start pouring in, just for the present the impecunious young couple could use a nice big influx of cash. The kind that only Daddy could supply.

They finally arrived at the trusty old homestead, and Jay's response to seeing the old pile was simply endearing.

"Jeez—exactly how rich are your parents?"

"Moderately rich," she said with a touch of satisfaction as she steered the car down the long drive, Twine Manor gleaming robust and proud in the distance.

"No, but I mean, are we talking millionaire or billionaire?"

"Not billionaire, I don't think," she said. She glanced over to her betrothed, giving him a critical once-over and trying to see him as her mother would. For the occasion she'd made him wear a decent pair of pants, and the nicest sweater in his possession. She'd even sent him to get a haircut, and he'd never looked better. With his natural boyish charm, and the floppy flair that was a hallmark of his artistic persona, and which had attracted her to him in the first place, she was absolutely convinced he would appeal to Mommy and Daddy.

Even before she'd rung the doorbell, the door swung open and the lady of the manor appeared, with Daddy by her side. They both seemed pleased to see her, but when they caught sight of Jay, that initial excitement quickly made place for a look of confusion.

"Mommy, Daddy," she said proudly, her voice wobbly with excitement, "I want you to meet Jay." She had planned to wait, but she was bubbling over with such a sense of pride that she suddenly blurted out, "We're engaged!" And with a flourish, she held up her hand, on which a very modest ring featured. It had belonged to Jay's mother, and was the best he could do on such short notice.

She'd pictured her parents' faces many times when confronted with the big news, though she had to admit that in her imagination they'd never looked like they did now. Instead of glowing with pride and effusively sharing her happiness, they looked stunned. Too stunned for speech, though that didn't take long.

Matilda Twine was the first to recover from the shock. "Have you lost your mind!" she screamed. Not exactly a ringing endorsement, as endorsements go.

Jay now stepped to the fore, anxious to make a good impression and possibly feeling that things weren't going according to plan. "My name is Jay Green," he said, with outstretched hand. "And can I say how happy I am to finally make your acquaintance?"

"You have got to be kidding," said Algis Twine. Like his wife, he now appeared intensely displeased with his daughter's surprise announcement.

"No, I'm not," said Laia. "Jay is my fiancé, and we're getting married."

"All I want to say is that—" said Jay, but Daddy talked right over him.

"He's an artist!" Daddy cried. "And a penniless artist, no less."

"He's not penniless," said Laia.

"He lives in a dump!"

Laia stared at her parent. "How do you know Jay is an artist, and how do you know where he lives?" And then the horrific truth came home to her. "Oh, my God! Have you been *spying* on me?!"

But Daddy waved her emotional outburst away. "He doesn't have a cent to his name. He doesn't even own the apartment where he lives, and it wouldn't surprise me if you've been using the rent we pay to support the both of you."

"You *have* been spying on me!"

"Of course we've been keeping an eye on you! What do you expect?"

"All I want to say," Jay repeated, "is that—"

"This is outrageous," said Laia. "You've actually gone and hired a detective?"

"A friend of ours had seen you," said Mommy. "In town, with this..." She gestured to Jay, giving him a distinct look of distaste. "This... loafer!"

"He's not a loafer," said Laia, crossing her arms in front of her chest. "Jay is a very talented artist, and what's more, he's my fiancé and we're in love."

"You must be mad," said Mommy in response. "Absolutely stark-raving mad!"

"Madly in love, you mean."

"Can I just say," said Jay, trying once more to put in his two cents. "That I love your daughter very much and—"

"He already has you living in that dump you call an apartment!" Mommy cried. "Between the cockroaches and the rats!"

"Like I said, Jay is an accomplished and very talented artist," said Laia. "And it won't be long before he makes a name for himself and breaks into the big time."

"Oh, honey, just dump the guy," said Daddy. "He's obviously a flake."

"He's not a flake!"

"I asked Martin, who owns a gallery on Hudson Street, and he says he's never even heard of the guy. And if Martin doesn't know him, I can tell you no one does."

"It's true that he isn't a household name yet," she admitted reluctantly, "but he will be once the world realizes what an amazing talent he is."

"He's a nobody!"

"Oh, honey, just snap out of it," said Mommy, "and move back home. This is just one of those things, don't you see?"

"Yeah, one of those phases," Daddy agreed.

"Look, can't we come in and talk about this like grownups?" she said, since they still hadn't moved past the threshold.

"*You* can come in," said Mommy, "but not... *him*."

"Jay is my fiancé," she insisted. "And I'm not going anywhere without him."

Jay cleared his throat. "I just want you to know how pleased I am to finally meet you, Mr. and Mrs. Twine, and I can assure you—"

"I'm afraid you'll have to choose, Laia," said Mommy, her expression hardening. "Either you come in alone, or you don't come in at all."

"Okay, so be it," said Laia, who could be as stubborn as her mother. "Then I won't come in."

"Fine," said Mommy.

"Fine," said Laia.

"Then I guess we're done here. Come, Algis."

And before Laia's astonished eyes, the door was slammed in her face!

Jay frowned. "What just happened?"

Laia took him by the arm, her initial disappointment and dismay quickly morphing into a sort of righteous rage. "I think they just kicked me out."

"Kicked you out? But they're your family."

"Yeah, well, looks like you're my family now."

She stared at the closed door for a few seconds more, vaguely hoping her parents would change their mind. But when that didn't happen, she gave the door a vicious kick, uttered a scream of frustration, then stomped off.

Once they were both inside her little car again, her future husband said, with a sort of stunned look on his face. "So now what?"

"Now we go home and start our life together," she said simply.

"But… what about your parents?"

She frowned at her childhood home, which all of a sudden had developed an air of foreboding. "I don't have parents anymore. From now on I'm an orphan."

*T*hey arrived home about twenty minutes later, to find that the postman had dumped another couple of parcels in the hallway.

"More junk we didn't order," said Jay, angrily checking the pile of boxes.

"And that we'll have to pay for with money we don't have," she said as she picked up a box with the logo of a familiar gaming company. "Have you filed a complaint with the police?"

"I have, but they didn't seem to take me seriously." He shook his head. "Who's doing this to us?"

"Could be my folks," she said slowly. It hadn't occurred to her before that they could be behind this recent deluge of unwanted and unsolicited parcels, but now it was obvious they might hate Jay so much they were trying to teach her a lesson.

Just then, the doorbell rang, and Jay uttered a curse. He yanked open the door. At his feet, a burning paper bag was lying.

"Christ," he said, and immediately started to stomp on it to put out the flames.

He probably shouldn't have done that, for the bag contained a pile of a sort of brownish substance that could only be described as excrement.

And as Jay stared at his shoe, now covered in the stuff, as was their doorstep, Laia knew for sure that this was her parents' doing.

In some kind of twisted joke, they'd put actual excrement all over Jay's nice shoes—the only pair of nice shoes he had.

Since it was now obvious her parents were completely out of control, something needed to be done, and quickly, too!

But what?

And as Jay tried to remove the smelly substance by scraping his shoe across the sidewalk, her eye suddenly fell on a copy of the *Hampton Cove Gazette*. On the front page, an article was printed about a recent murder case that had taken place at some swanky hotel in Paris. The authoress appeared to have solved the murder, together with her husband, who was a cop. And as she scanned the article, she remembered how Dan Goory had once said Odelia Kingsley was simply the best.

And suddenly she knew exactly what to do.

CHAPTER 2

𝓘t had been a pretty busy time for us, and so when the opportunity arose for me to take a prolonged nap, I didn't hesitate and took it. One learns from these experiences, you see. When one is adopted by a woman who fashions herself to be a reporter-slash-sleuth and is married to a cop, it's imperative one learns to take the rough with the smooth, and take one's naps whenever and wherever one can.

In other words: I was tired so I slept. And I would have slept more, if Harriet hadn't decided to stir me from my slumber.

"Max," she said, shaking me when I didn't immediately react. "Max, hellooo!"

Of course she had me at hello, but I decided to ignore her, hoping she'd soon go away. When that didn't work, I finally yawned and said, "What?" Hoping to convey the sentiment that I'd rather be left in peace, you know. A sort of gentle hint, if you will. A subtle reminder of the sacredness of nap time. Unfortunately Harriet isn't one for subtlety, or for taking hints.

Instead she gave me a beaming smile and said, "Look!"

I looked, and when I didn't see, I said, more or less unhappily, "What is it I'm supposed to be looking at?"

"My painting, of course!"

"Painting? What painting?"

"I've made a new painting!" she said, still with that pretty excitement that has made her so popular with a certain type of male.

This time I decided to look where she was pointing, and lo and behold, she had indeed created a new chapter in her career as a budding *artiste*.

Next to me, my friend Dooley also stirred. "What's going on?" he asked, only now becoming aware of these exciting goings-on in our backyard.

"Harriet has made a new painting," I said. "And she wants us to take a look."

"Oh," said Dooley, without much enthusiasm. You see, Harriet has been trying to get her career going for quite a while now, and the problem is that when an artist sets out to make the world a better place by spreading some sweetness and light by honing their craft, at first they are simply not very good. It takes time to become a better artist, and in some cases a lot of time indeed.

But all the while, the beginning artist insists on imposing on their nearest and dearest with the imperfect products of their newfound hobby. So imperfect, in fact, that it hurts the eyes just having to look at the stuff.

In Harriet's case it didn't help that she'd picked paw-painting as her art of choice. It's like finger-painting, you see, only with paws, since cats don't have fingers, per se. Basically she dips her paws in paint and applies them to canvas.

It's fun, it's easy, and the results aren't always to write home about.

The painting Harriet had thusly created essentially

consisted of blots and splashes. I guess it was art of some kind, though of course I'm not an expert.

"Very nice," I murmured as I regarded our friend's latest creation.

"It's very... colorful?" Dooley tried.

Harriet regarded us sternly. Clearly such half-hearted praise would not do.

"Nice? Colorful?" she said. "Is that the best you can do? Don't you mean earth-shatteringly innovative? Stunningly creative? Stupefyingly amazing?"

"Absolutely," I quickly said. "All of that and more, I'm sure."

"Mh," she said, giving me a distinctly critical look. "Brutus!" she bellowed, waking up her loyal mate. "What do you think?"

"It's wonderful, sugar plum," the black cat rasped sleepily. "Absolutely gorgeous." He opened his eyes. "What am I looking at?" And when Harriet pointed toward her painting with a sort of indulgent smile, I could see how Brutus winced a little, but then managed to plaster a sufficiently appreciative expression onto his mug. "Great stuff!" he finally croaked, but he couldn't stop one eyelid from trembling at being subjected to such a smorgasbord of riotous color. It's one thing to practice the novel art of paw-painting, but it's quite another to do it well, and I think it's safe to say that Harriet hadn't yet moved past the novice stage.

She now frowned. "One problem I seem to be facing is that paint is so hard to get off. Just look at my paws." She held up her paws, which usually are a pristine white, but were now covered in a smattering of color.

I staggered back at the sight. No cat enjoys the prospect of getting even a teensy tiny bit of dirt on their coat. It's a matter of pride to be clean. And now this!

"Harriet, that's terrible!" I cried. And I wasn't even referring to her painting.

"Yeah, how are you going to get that off?" asked Brutus with a frown of concern.

"Oh, stop fussing," said Harriet. "It's just paint. The lifeblood of my art."

"Better be careful," I warned her. "Some of these paints are poisonous."

"Yeah, some of it is full of lead," Brutus added as he regarded his beloved nervously for signs of lead disease.

"I'm sure Odelia wouldn't buy *that* kind of paint," Harriet said dismissively. "She's a responsible pet parent, and would never put me in harm's way."

"Still," I said. I suddenly found myself wondering about the dangers of art. Hadn't I heard stories about artists who'd died destitute and in ill health? Some of them living in the gutter? Maybe toxic paint was a factor in these situations.

"You're absolutely right," said Harriet after I'd relayed my concerns.

"I am?" I said, much surprised. It's a rare thing when Harriet agrees with me on anything. Secretly, of course, I was hoping she'd give up painting, which would certainly be beneficial to our mental health.

"And so I've decided that from now on *you're* going to do the actual painting!" As she spoke these words, she was directing a proud look at Brutus.

At first, our friend didn't respond. I don't think he'd actually realized the implications of Harriet's words, to be honest. But when he finally did, he gave me a startled look, then said, in a sort of hoarse whisper, "What, me?!"

"Yes, you. You're a terrific artist, Brutus, and I'm going to prove it. Under my guidance you'll become almost as good as me." And she beamed upon him with pride, not unlike a parent looks upon a favorite, even though dimwitted, child.

"But… I can't paint!" Brutus cried.

"Of course you can paint. Anyone can paint. Now get off your tush and let's get to work!"

CHAPTER 3

And while Harriet was grooming her newly discovered assistant and a new burgeoning talent was about to be unleashed upon an unsuspecting world, we decided to look for our peace and quiet elsewhere. And that's how we arrived in the next-door backyard where we came upon Marge, our human's beloved mom.

Oddly enough, Marge didn't look her customary relaxed self. She wasn't reading a hefty page-turner in one of the lounge chairs positioned there just for that purpose. Instead, she was standing behind what looked like an easel, squinting at it with a sort of pensive look in the one eye that was still open.

"What's that in her hand, Max?" asked Dooley in a sort of hushed tone.

"If I'm not mistaken, Dooley," I said, studying the object under discussion more closely, "I think that's called a brush. And it's commonly used to paint things."

"Paint what?" he asked.

"Well, I would assume she's painting something on the canvas she's staring at."

"I don't get it," said Dooley. "I thought Marge was a librarian, not a painter?"

"If Harriet is to be believed, anyone can paint, Dooley, even librarians."

We circled the entrancing scene, careful not to disturb Marge, who was obviously in the throes of some artistic mood. Once we caught sight of the canvas, I saw she was painting what looked like a tree. Or at least as much like a tree as can be accepted, taking a liberty with the limitations of the physical universe.

"What are you doing, Marge?" Dooley asked, for he, too, must have wondered why anyone would paint a sort of green blob on top of a sort of brownish blob.

Marge jerked out of her trance, and in doing so, liberally spilled drops of paint all over myself and Dooley.

"Yikes!" I cried as the noxious substance hit my smooth blorange coat.

"Oh, I'm so sorry, Max!" Marge said, as she hastened to wipe away the spillage with a rag. Unfortunately the rag was dirtier than the brush had been, and so she only managed to make even more of a mess, if that was possible.

It took her a little while to undo the damage, but when we looked more or less spic and span again, Dooley repeated his question: "What are you doing?"

"I'm painting," said Marge lightly, as if that hadn't been obvious from the first.

"What are you painting?" asked Dooley. "Except us, I mean."

Marge gave my friend a puzzled frown. "Why, a tree, of course. Isn't it obvious?"

Dooley studied the work of art some more, then finally shook his head. "It doesn't look like a tree," he said honestly.

"Well, that's because this is just a preliminary study," said

Marge, regarding her own work with a touch of doubtfulness. "Once I finish, the real work begins."

"And why are you painting trees?" asked Dooley, continuing his third degree.

Marge shrugged. "Because I like it. It's very relaxing to paint, you know."

I thought back to Brutus and the horrified expression on his face when Harriet announced that from now on he was an artist. Somehow I didn't associate art with relaxation. Then again, maybe it's different for humans. Oftentimes they find joy in the most peculiar pastimes. Like hiking in nature. Or riding a bicycle.

Just then, Odelia came wandering into the backyard, hoisting Grace in her arms. The latter was gazing around herself with a sort of curious look on her face, as if wondering what all the fuss was about.

"Oh, hey, honey," said Marge. "I've been meaning to ask you. Do you want to join me for art class tonight? It's a lot more fun if I bring a friend."

"I'm sorry, but I can't, Mom," said Odelia. "I've got an article to finish and it can't wait."

"Mh," said Marge, looking slightly disappointed. Ever since Odelia had started work again, her leisure time was limited. She'd always been a busy bee, and now with a baby to take care of, her spare time was even more at a premium than before.

"Why don't you ask Gran? I'm sure she'd love to go."

Marge grimaced. Obviously the notion of taking her mother along with her to this art class didn't appeal to her as much as it should have.

"Love to go where?" asked Gran. She came walking out of the house, wearing brown tennis shoes and a fluorescent green tracksuit, a combination which was oddly compatible with Marge's tree.

"Art class," said Odelia before Marge could shut her up. "Mom doesn't feel like going all by herself, and I'm busy tonight, so we were wondering if you wanted to go."

"Art class? What are you talking about?" asked Gran, as she cast a skeptical glance at her daughter's latest creation.

"The library is organizing an art exhibition with works of people from Hampton Cove," Marge explained, "so I thought why not join the fun and create something myself?"

"How many lessons have you had?" asked Gran as she leaned in and studied the painting, then stepped back and studied it some more, looking very much like an art critic in the way she was cupping her chin and frowning critically.

"One," said Marge. "I was supposed to go with Margaret Samson, but she canceled at the last minute and now I'm looking—"

"What is that thing, I wonder," said Gran.

Marge set her teeth. "It's a tree. In fact it's that tree over there." She pointed to one of the trees that line the back of the garden.

Gran's face cleared. "Oh, so that's what it is. Well, I'd say keep practicing, honey. You're not quite there yet."

"It's just a preliminary study," Dooley explained. "Once this is done the real work begins."

"Is that a fact?" said Gran with a grin, and started to walk away.

"Oh, Gran, can you take care of Grace? I have to run down to the office."

"Sure thing," said Gran, and took Grace over from Odelia, gently rubbing the little one's back. She headed back inside. "We're going to have a great time together, you and I," she told her great-granddaughter. "Oh, yes, we will."

"So, Gran, how about it?" said Odelia.

"How about what?" asked the old lady, turning back with a quizzical look.

"Can you join Mom for her art class?"

"No can do, I'm afraid," said Gran.

"I didn't know you had something else going on."

"I have nothing going on. But we all know that art is for suckers. See ya."

And then she was gone.

Dooley turned to me. "What does she mean, Max? Why is art for suckers?"

"You'd have to ask her, Dooley," I said.

"I'll show her what art can do," said Marge. "I'm going to make the best painting in that exhibit, or my name isn't Marge Poole."

"That's the spirit, Mom," said Odelia, giving her mother an encouraging smile. "And for what it's worth, I think your tree looks very much like a tree. Absolutely."

"Thanks, honey. It's just a preliminary study, though. Once I get going, I'm sure it's going to look even more like a tree."

"Why did Marge say her name isn't Marge Poole, Max?" asked Dooley. "Has she changed her name?"

"I think you'll find that she said her name *is* Marge Poole," I said, "and because it is, she's going to create a very nice painting for her exhibit."

"Oh," said my friend, then turned to Marge, arguably the best source of information on all things Marge Poole. "Marge, is your name still Marge or have you changed it?"

But Marge wasn't listening. Not when she was on the verge of creating art with a capital A. So she simply ignored us and continued painting a preliminary tree.

We watched on for several more minutes, while Marge chatted with her daughter. I could tell that the artist's heart wasn't really in it, though. Women are great at multitasking, of course, but there are limits. And clearly this limit was reached when she finally said, "Didn't you say you had to go to the office, hon?"

It was a subtle reminder, as reminders go, but it was clear enough in its simplicity. Odelia sort of seemed to collect herself, and then she was off. But not before turning to us and saying, "Max, Dooley, are you coming?"

Looked like nap-time was over.

CHAPTER 4

As usual I'd taken too gloomy a view of my prospects. The moment we arrived, I rediscovered our cozy little nook in Odelia's office, and soon I was soundly asleep once more. In fact this was probably an even better solution, since there were no would-be artists who could interrupt my peaceful slumber there.

And as Odelia went back to work, first stretching, then focusing on her article, I heaved a sigh of utter contentment, and the moment her fingers hit the keyboard and that sweet melody of typing was floating through the air, I was already in the land of dreams—and I didn't even need to make a preliminary study to create my own dreamscape.

But of course these rare moments of absolute bliss never last. A knock sounded at the door, and a couple strode in, desiring speech with our human.

I yawned and placed my head on my front paws to take in these new arrivals. They were both young, dressed in simple jeans and matching sweaters. The woman was pretty in a sort of understated way, but the man had a shaggy mane, and some patchy growth on his chin, and reminded me of... an artist!

"Who are these people, Max?" asked Dooley, who'd been enjoying his own version of the perfect nap right next to me.

"I have no idea, Dooley," I said. "But I have a feeling we're going to find out."

"Oh, hi," said Odelia, looking up from her work. When she's in the middle of an article you can practically fire off a canon next to her, and she won't even notice.

"Hi," said the young woman, taking the lead. "I hope we're not interrupting? Mr. Goory told us to walk right through."

"Oh, no, it's fine," said Odelia, and closed her laptop. "What can I do for you?"

"Well, um..." said the girl, with a touch of hesitation. It's never a lot of fun to lay one's private matters at the feet of a total stranger, but then Odelia, being the *Hampton Cove Gazette's* main reporter, and also its editorialist, is of course a familiar face to most people, even if they're not always a familiar face to her.

"There isn't much I haven't heard before, trust me," said Odelia encouragingly.

The young man cleared his throat. "I'm Jay," he said. "Jay Green. And this is Laia, my fiancée. And we're the target of some kind of harassment campaign."

"Harassment?" asked Odelia, her interest piqued. "You mean like a stalker?"

"Yeah, I guess you could say that."

"Someone is sending us stuff we didn't order," the man's fiancée explained. "Expensive stuff. And then of course these companies expect us to pay for it."

"These people, whoever they are," said Jay, "apparently create an account in my name, and just keep ordering all kinds of things. And then when I refuse to pay, the companies come after me, wanting their money. I keep telling them it wasn't me that ordered it, but more often than not they don't believe me."

"It's a nightmare," Laia said. "We've received dozens and dozens of deliveries, and the bills are piling up. Bills for things we don't want and don't need."

"Can't you go to the police?" asked Odelia. "File a complaint?"

"Oh, I did," said Jay, "and they took down my statement."

"But that's all they've done so far," said Laia. "They're in no hurry to go after these people, even though it just keeps getting worse day by day."

"This morning two laptops arrived," said Jay. "As well as three mattresses and a cross trainer. I told them to take it all back, but they refused. Said they were just the delivery people, and I had to take it up with the store."

"And yesterday, a pile of doo-doo was on our doorstep," said Laia. "Probably dog doo-doo. It was in a paper bag, which had been set on fire."

"I stepped in it, trying to put out the fire," said Jay sadly.

"The same people, you think?" asked Odelia, who'd started jotting down notes.

Jay shrugged. "Impossible to say. Though it wouldn't surprise me."

"And then there's the gigolo thing," said Laia. She gave her fiancé a gentle nudge. "Tell her about the gigolo thing, Jay."

"Gigolo thing?" asked Odelia.

Jay shuffled uncomfortably in his chair. "Yeah, see, the thing is, someone must have signed me up for a dating site, cause I keep getting calls and messages from older women trying to engage my... services."

"Here," said Laia, holding out a phone. "This is one of the messages Jay got this morning."

Odelia frowned at the phone and read, "Hey, handsome. Are you free for some fun time tonight? I'm a hot young bombshell looking for a good time. Call me. Scarlett... Canyon?" She suppressed a smile as she handed back the phone.

"Is Scarlett a hot young bombshell, Max?" asked Dooley.

"I guess in her own mind she is," I said.

"So you see?" said Laia. "This keeps on happening, and it has got to stop."

"Yeah, I can see how it might be annoying," Odelia agreed. "How long has this been going on?"

The young couple shared a look. "About... a month now?" Jay ventured.

"It all started right after I moved in with Jay," Laia explained. "Which probably is no coincidence. You see, my parents don't approve of our relationship. And they've hired a private detective to keep tabs on me. So it wouldn't surprise me if they're behind this terrible business."

"You don't know that," said Jay.

"I wouldn't put it past them," said Laia. She turned back to Odelia. "Jay and I recently got engaged, and so I decided to introduce him to my parents and give them the good news. Only they freaked out and more or less threw me out."

"Talk about a car crash," Jay said sadly.

"Yeah, they pretty much cut me off," said Laia. "Which is why I think it might be them. Trying to put pressure on me to dump Jay." She clasped her fiancé's arm. "Which I will never, ever do. We're in love, and they'll just have to accept it."

"Okay, so did you talk to your parents about this?" asked Odelia. "The online orders, the flaming paper bag, the, um, gigolo thing?"

"I called Mommy, but she's blocking my calls, and so is

Daddy. So finally I dropped by the house, but they refused to let me in, or even to see me."

"So you can't be sure your parents are behind this?"

"No, but who else could it be?"

"We did say it might be Bud," said Jay quietly.

"Bud wouldn't do this," said Laia. "He's not crazy. Bud is my ex-boyfriend," she explained. "He took it pretty hard when I broke up with him." She darted a quick glance at her fiancé. "Or what about Loretta?"

But Jay shook his head determinedly. "Not a chance."

"Who's Loretta?" asked Odelia.

"My ex-girlfriend," said Jay. "But I'm sure she's got nothing to do with this."

"Yeah, well, I don't think we should rule her out," said Laia. She gave Odelia a hopeful look. "So can you help us, Mrs. Kingsley? Dan said you're simply the best."

"He said that, did he?" said Odelia laughingly. "Do you know Dan?"

"He's a friend of the family."

"Of course he is," said Odelia as she tapped a thoughtful pencil against her notebook. Then she tore off a page and placed it before the young woman. "Can you write down the names and information of the people you just mentioned? Your ex-boyfriend, Jay's ex-girlfriend... and your parents, of course."

Laia's face lit up with delight. "So you'll take the case?"

"I'll take the case," said Odelia, and I could tell she was more than a little bit intrigued. As was I, I have to admit. I mean, what's not to like? Mysterious packages, flaming paper bags containing dog doo-doo, and of course hot young bombshells who turn out to be Gran's best friend Scarlett Canyon? Bring it on.

Dutifully Laia jotted down the names and contact details

of the people she thought might be doing this to her and her fiancé, and handed it to Odelia.

Her only stipulation, when Jay mentioned fees, was that she could turn this into an article for the paper once the culprit was caught. And an interesting article it would be. Human interest and all that. Though it had stirred my feline interest, too.

CHAPTER 5

Odelia actually felt disproportionally glad that Jay and Laia had walked into the office. Ever since she'd had Grace, her usual workload had slackened to some extent, and to be honest she'd felt a little bored sitting at home and not being able to tackle a really juicy case the way she was used to.

And even though this case wasn't exactly the biggest case she'd ever handled, it still inspired her to go out there and do her bit for the sake of a young couple's future happiness. And if she could squeeze a great story out of it, even better.

So it was with a spring in her step that she breezed into the Hampton Cove police precinct and strode up to the reception desk. If it was true what Laia said and the police had given them the runaround, she wanted to know why that was.

Behind her, Max and Dooley had hardly been able to keep up, but they still tried, since it was obvious that they, too, were chomping at the bit to dig their teeth into a nice fat case again.

"Hey, honey," Dolores rasped. The crusty receptionist

wasn't actually smoking a cigarette at that exact moment, but she had all the hallmarks of a woman who had just smoked one, smoker's voice and all. "What brings you here?"

"I just had a young couple in my office who claim they've filed a complaint and were given the runaround by you," said Odelia, not beating about the bush.

"Is that a fact?" said Dolores, not impressed. "Who's the couple?"

"Jay Green and Laia Twine. They've been getting parcels sent to them that they didn't order, and Jay's name is out there advertising him as a gigolo, when he's anything but." She gave Dolores a quizzical look. "Any of that ring a bell?"

"Yeah, now that you mention it, I think it does," she said, nodding. "Handsome young guy? The artistic type?"

"Yep, that's him."

"Honey, they're yanking your chain. The guy is obviously a gigolo, only he's afraid to tell his girl, and so he made up this cockamamie story about a stalker being after him or whatever."

"So what about these shipments that keep arriving? All of it stuff they never ordered but are expected to pay for?"

"Nonsense. Did you take a good look at the guy? I'm sure he's very successful at what he does, and so the women who pay for his services send him tons of gifts. Nothing wrong with that."

"What's wrong is that these companies are expecting him to pay."

But Dolores didn't look convinced. "Oh, come on. That's the story he's been telling his girl. Of course he can't admit he's been getting gifts from his clients, so he made up this cock and bull story about some stalker." She shrugged her bony shoulders, almost pulling them up to her ears. "Let her figure it out for herself is what I say. If she wants to be hoodwinked by her boyfriend, that's her business."

"He also mentioned something about a paper bag of doo-doo on his doorstep."

Dolores laughed a raspy laugh. "One of his clients must be really unhappy with him, huh! Guess he didn't give her what she wanted. Happens all the time." And then she laughed some more, the story obviously having tickled her funny bone. When she saw that Odelia wasn't joining in the merriment, she finally pulled herself together and wiped the tears from her eyes. "Look, if you want my advice, I'd tell the kid to come clean. The sooner he does, the better. And if this girl really loves him, she'll forgive him. And if not? Well, he's only got himself to blame, right?"

Just then, the phone belted out a musical tone, and she held up a finger as she picked up. Looked like the conversation was over.

Odelia turned away and glanced in the direction of the swinging door that led to the heart of the police precinct. Should she bother her uncle with this? Or Chase? But then she decided not to. If what Dolores said was the official police line, they weren't going to be much help. And besides, this was her case. Her story, and she had to decide if Jay Green was a gigolo and a liar, or if he was for real, and he did indeed have a stalker issue.

So instead of barging into her uncle's office, she headed back out, two cats hot on her tail.

"What did she say?" asked Dooley. "Why didn't she take Laia's story seriously?"

"Dolores thinks that Jay really is a gigolo," she said as she stood conferring with herself on the sidewalk, figuring out her next course of action.

Dooley promptly turned to Max. "What's a gigolo, Max?"

"Um..." was Max's eloquent response. "Well..." He gave Odelia a strained look.

She crouched down and tickled Dooley under the chin.

"A gigolo is a man who keeps lonely women company," she explained. "Women who have no husband but still want to enjoy the company of a man, and so they pay him for the privilege."

"Oh, so he's like a nurse?"

She grimaced. "Yeah, something like that."

Max mouthed, 'Thank you,' and she gave him a wink.

CHAPTER 6

Bud Zuk, Laia's ex-boyfriend, turned out to be the tennis pro at our local tennis club. He was certainly dressed like a tennis pro, in white tennis shorts and shirt, swinging his tennis racket like he meant business. He also had one of those funny wristbands on his left wrist, but I saw that his right wrist was bandaged up.

"Had an accident?" Odelia asked the moment we sat down with the guy in the club canteen.

He held up the damaged appendage and studied it for a moment, as if contemplating an alien object. Finally he said, "Just a light sprain. The doc says it should be fine in no time. And I intend to hold him to that promise!" He laughed, flashing two rows of perfect white teeth.

All in all he was a very attractive young man, fully tanned and looking very fit.

"I don't think he sprained that arm, Max," said Dooley, who sat next to me underneath Odelia's chair. We'd both tucked in our tails, so as not to make them a prime target for any passersby. Humans do love to trample on a cat's tail, you see. Must be some innate taste for the sadistic.

"You don't?" I asked.

"I think he burned it when he was putting that burning bag of dog doo-doo on Laia and Jay's porch."

"It's possible," I conceded.

"By the way, how do we know that doo-doo belonged to a dog?" my friend now added to his musings. "It could have been cat doo-doo."

"Considering there was a lot of it," I said, "it's safe to assume that excrement was of canine origin. Cats don't produce that much, you see."

"It could have been human doo-doo. Humans produce a lot of doo-doo."

"That's true," I admitted. "Humans are indeed big doo-doo producers."

"They should have taken a DNA test down at the station when Jay brought the doo-doo in for questioning."

"I don't think he ever did take the bag into the police station," I said. "And he certainly didn't take it in for questioning, Dooley. I mean, how does one question a bag of doo-doo, whether human, canine or feline?"

"No, I see your point," he conceded. "It's hard to question doo-doo, isn't it?"

But the notion of taking a DNA sample was a valid point, and one I made a mental note of to relay to Odelia once this interview was over. If Laia and Jay had kept the bag as evidence, of course, which might not be the case.

"So you've been talking to Laia, huh?" said the tennis pro, casually leaning back and nursing a soda. He smiled a wistful smile. "How is she these days? Doing well, I trust?"

"Like I said, she's the victim of a harassment campaign," Odelia reminded him.

"Yeah, you mentioned that," said the pro. Then he frowned, and it was obvious that the penny had finally dropped. "She's not accusing *me*, is she?"

"She mentioned you in passing," said Odelia smoothly. "She claims you took it pretty hard when the relationship ended."

"Well, she's right about that. I did take it pretty hard." He shrugged. "Then again, these things happen, and I've put the whole thing behind me. I mean, did I think we were meant to be together? Sure. Absolutely. Which just goes to show: you just never know. But life will throw you these curveballs sometimes."

"Had you been together long?"

"Didn't she tell you? Laia and I have known each other since we were kids. Our parents are best friends, you see. Have been for years. My dad is president of the club, and Laia's dad is his treasurer. And I guess they thought we'd end up together one day, and when we did, it made the old buzzards very happy."

"But it wasn't to be."

"No, it wasn't to be. Jay Green arrived on the scene, and Laia took a shine to him, and suddenly her childhood friend was old news." He spoke with a touch of bitterness, I noticed, even though he tried to keep his tone light and cheerful.

"So how do you feel about Jay?" asked Odelia.

"Oh, I think he's probably a great guy, and a great artist, otherwise Laia wouldn't have chosen him as her boyfriend. But apart from that..." He toyed with a paper umbrella that someone had left on the table in front of him. "Look, I don't really know the guy, okay? We don't exactly move in the same circles."

"How did Laia and Jay meet? Do you know?"

"No, to be honest I don't. One day she just told me out of the blue that she'd met this artist fellow and that she was breaking up with me, and that was that."

"That must have upset you a great deal."

He flashed her another smile. "It was a painful experience,

but that doesn't mean I'm going to turn psycho and start harassing them. I'm not that kind of guy."

"You're sure you didn't leave a bag of flaming... excrement on your ex-girlfriend's doorstep?"

He shook his head decidedly. "Absolutely not. Such poor taste."

"Or sign Jay up for a dating site, promoting him as some kind of gigolo?"

This time he actually laughed out loud. "Oh, my God, that's the funniest thing I ever heard! That actually happened?"

"Yes, it did. Jay gets messages and calls from strange women, wanting to engage his services."

He gave Odelia a clever look. "Are you sure he's not secretly a gigolo, and when Laia found out he made up this story about being harassed?"

"That's what the police think," Odelia admitted. "But not what Laia believes."

He took another sip from his drink. "She always was too naive for her own good. I'll bet you this guy Jay is bad news, and now that Laia is caught in his web, he'll do anything to keep her." He arched a meaningful eyebrow. "Her family is loaded, you know. Her parents made their money by launching one of the first online gambling sites. Last I heard they're billionaires. And I don't know if this is a coincidence or not, but Jay Green popped onto the scene exactly one week after *Time Magazine* devoted an article to Algis Twine, calling him the original cyberbillionaire, long before anyone had even heard of such a thing."

"So you think Jay is stringing Laia along."

He held up his hands. "Awfully big coincidence, wouldn't you say?"

"Okay, but let's assume for a moment that Jay isn't a gigolo, and that he really is the victim of a harassment campaign. Can you think of anyone who could be behind this?"

He drew a wrinkle between his brows for a moment, then nodded thoughtfully. "Have you talked to Loretta Everyman?"

Odelia consulted her notes. "Jay's ex-girlfriend?"

"Yeah. Real piece of work. Real skank, if you catch my drift."

"How do you know so much about Jay?"

That clever look was back. "The moment Laia told me she had a new boyfriend, I made it my business to find out more about him. Laia has always been my best friend, Mrs. Kingsley, and even though she broke up with me, that doesn't change the way I feel about her. Look, frankly I was worried about her. I still am."

"So you hired a private detective to spy on Jay?"

"No, nothing like that. I just asked around, and let me tell you: the stories I heard weren't good. But when I confronted Laia with them, she said I was just being jealous. So for my own sense of self-preservation I decided to step back."

"Very noble of you."

"I know," he said, not catching the irony. "But hey, even though I adopted a hands-off approach, I still worry. How can I not? I care for Laia. Always have, always will." He nodded. "She's a great gal, and Jay Green doesn't deserve her."

CHAPTER 7

"For a man who says he has no hard feelings toward his ex-girlfriend Bud sure has a lot of hard feelings toward his ex-girlfriend," Dooley remarked as we climbed back into Odelia's battered old pickup.

"You're right about that, Dooley," said Odelia as she tapped her keys against the steering wheel. She turned to us. "So what did you think? Could he be involved? Or is Jay hoodwinking his girlfriend, like Bud says?"

"Hard to tell," I said. "One thing's for sure, Bud holds a serious grudge against Jay."

"Yeah, I got that impression, too."

"I don't think he was being fair," said Dooley. "A gigolo provides a very important service to humanity. With all those lonely women out there, it's very decent and very kind of him to provide some company to all those ladies."

I shared a smile with Odelia. "It's not a given that Jay really is a gigolo," said Odelia. "He claims he isn't, so there's that."

"He's probably one of those discreet benefactors," said

Dooley. "Who do a lot of good but don't want people to know about it. You know, like a modern saint."

This time Odelia actually had to laugh, earning her a confused look from Dooley.

"We better have a chat with this..." She consulted her notes again. "Um, Loretta Everyman."

"What's a skank, Odelia?" asked Dooley, without missing a beat. "Is that like a skunk? Cause I saw a documentary about skunks on the Discovery Channel and when they get scared they spray you with something very smelly."

"A skank is a not-so-pleasant person," I said. "Perhaps a little sleazy."

"Do you think Loretta Everyman will spray us with something very smelly when she doesn't like us? Cause I just finished grooming myself, you know."

"No, I don't think Loretta will spray us with something smelly," I said.

Odelia cranked her car in gear and backed out from between a Tesla and a BMW. These tennis club people sure had a lot of money to spend on cars.

"Maybe one of these days you should buy yourself a new car," I suggested, not for the first time.

"Yeah, I guess you're right," she said with a sigh. Then had to use all her strength to yank hard at the wheel, making sure she didn't hit a nice Porsche.

I guess back when they made her pickup—in the Stone Age, I mean—they hadn't invented power steering yet, and expected people to develop extra muscles to make their cars go where they wanted them to go. Then again, Odelia is plenty strong. If you can squeeze an entire infant out of your tummy, you have to be.

. . .

*L*oretta Everyman worked the counter at our local supermarket. No, not the General Store, where our friend Kingman is more or less in charge, but the supermarket located in the strip mall on the road into town.

Loretta was hard at work sliding her customers' wares along the scanner when we approached.

"Could I have a quick word, perhaps?" Odelia suggested, placing a can of cat food on the counter, which was an excellent choice indeed. "Jay Green told me to talk to you," she clarified when Loretta stared at her, uncomprehending. At the mention of her ex-boyfriend, a sort of dark cloud slid across the young woman's face and she grunted, "I have no idea who that is." She picked up the can of cat food, scanned it and slammed it down again. "That'll be one ninety-nine."

"Jay is the victim of a harassment campaign," Odelia explained as she took out her card.

"Oh, and he thinks I had something to do with that, does he? Well, that's just great."

"I'm not saying you're the person responsible," said Odelia, talking quickly, since a line was forming behind her. "Just that maybe you could shed some light on who is."

"Look, all I know is that Jay's trouble started when he hooked up with that Laia person. So whatever is going on, he only has himself to blame."

"And why is that?"

Loretta gave Odelia a not-so-friendly look. "Who are you? A cop?"

"Not a cop, no. Laia and Jay asked me to investigate, so that's what I'm doing."

"You know who Laia Twine is, don't you?"

Odelia merely waited, which is a great technique for getting people to talk.

Loretta heaved an exaggerated sigh. "Look, the only

reason Jay dumped me is because Laia is this little rich girl, and since he's basically a failure as an artist, he probably hoped she would bankroll his lifestyle. Set him up in a studio of his own, where he can tinker and mess around without actually having to make any money. Only from what I'm hearing, her parents cut her off the moment she tried to foist Jay on them. So now they're both in big trouble."

"So you're saying the only reason Jay dumped you is because Laia is rich?"

"Sure! We had a good thing going, me and Jay. Or at least I thought we had. But then Miss Moneybags came along, and suddenly I wasn't good enough for the Starving Artist."

"You wouldn't happen to have created a profile for Jay on a dating site, would you?"

"No, I would not," said Loretta decidedly. "Now if you'll excuse me, people are waiting."

And so it became clear that our interview was at an end.

Once outside, Dooley said with a sort of puzzled look on his face, "She didn't look sleazy to me, Max. Her clothes were clean, her face was washed, and she smelled nice."

"Yeah, I think Bud Zuk wasn't being very nice when he made that comment," I agreed. "She looks like a very nice girl." A little resentful, perhaps, but that was to be expected, if what she said about Jay was true.

We all piled into the pickup again, and Odelia voiced the general sentiment when she said, "So now what?"

"Now we know that Jay's ex-girlfriend and Laia's ex-boyfriend both claim they have nothing to do with this stalking business," I said. "Which either means that one of them is a liar, or that the real culprit is to be found elsewhere."

"I think it's the parents," said Dooley. "They obviously hate Jay for taking their girl away from them, and they're trying to make her give him up."

"It's possible," Odelia conceded. She checked her clock. "We better leave Mr. and Mrs. Twine for tomorrow, though."

I eyed that can of cat food with a distinct sense of relish. It was the cheap store brand kind of stuff, but it still looked tasty enough. "Excellent idea," I murmured.

CHAPTER 8

Brutus wasn't in the best mood he could have been. Harriet had him paw-painting, which apparently was a new technique, reminiscent of finger-painting, something young humans excelled at, and it was taking a toll on his peace of mind.

In general he didn't mind Harriet's capricious nature, or even the fact that she got these weird brainstorms from time to time and insisted on carrying them out with or without his assistance, but he drew the line at making an absolute and complete fool of himself, as he was sure he was doing now!

"Paw-painting, if you please," he murmured darkly to himself. Once more he dabbed a paw into one of the many buckets of paint Harriet had asked Gran to put at her disposal and applied it to the large piece of paper Harriet had positioned on the lawn for the purpose of furthering her art.

"Not bad, Brutus!" Harriet yelled from the sidelines. "A little more to the right. Now just draw a straight line all the way… a *straight* line, Brutus! That's crooked!"

"Yeah, yeah, yeah," he muttered. "It's not so easy to draw a straight line!" he said, a little louder. And definitely when you didn't have the overview, like Harriet.

She'd taken position on a chair and was having a bird's eye view, so to speak.

"I don't think I like what you're doing, Brutus," she now yelled as she watched him with a touch of dubiousness. "Those greens and those reds don't mix!"

Brutus glanced down at his paws, which were a many-colored miasma of smelly paint. It was going to prove a real difficulty to get it off.

"Try the yellow," Harriet now suggested. "Just a little bit of yellow up there in the corner." She was pointing in the general direction of the side of the painting he'd hoped he was done with, since he'd already turned it into a veritable smorgasbord of riotous color, and each time he walked in it, it added to the mess.

But yellow it had to be, so yellow it was.

He carefully dipped his left paw into the bucket of paint, and then sort of hobbled in the direction Harriet had indicated and daubed it on the canvas.

"Much, much better!" Harriet said, much to his elation. "You did it, cookie jar. It's shaping up really well, don't you think?"

He eyed her stoically. "Absolutely," he said, even though he had absolutely no idea what he was doing, apart from getting his paws dirty, of course.

"Better come up here," Harriet suggested. "So you can see what I did."

What she did? What he did, she meant. But still he did as he was told, and joined her on the chair, taking in the scenery. To him it just looked like a big mess.

"See what I was trying to do there?" asked Harriet, as she studied the work of art with a critical eye. "The breadth of incarnation and the whimsy of adhering to a strict delineation inherited down the ages is perfectly reflected in the daring touches as applied with a bold and deft flourish by an artist's innate folly."

He had absolutely no idea what she just said, but as long as it meant that he was done, he was all for it. "Absolutely," he said therefore. "Just what I thought."

Harriet beamed upon him with an expansive smile. "Brutus, my dear heart, I think we've just created my very first masterpiece! Hurray!"

"Hurray indeed," he echoed.

Inside the house, Gran was holding Grace, gently rocking her in her arms. She was staring out the kitchen window, wondering what it was that Harriet thought she and Brutus were doing. When Harriet had asked for supplies to start her budding artist's career, she hadn't thought much of it. Cats are funny creatures, and Harriet took the cake when it came to eccentricity sometimes. But painting? Then again, if Bob Ross was to be believed, anyone could paint, so why not cats? And she had to admit there was something soothing about watching a cat paint.

Maybe she could make a video and post it on YouTube. God knows people could use something uplifting in their lives.

She turned away from the window and returned to the living room, where she proceeded to cast one eye on the television, and a second eye on her smartphone to see if Scarlett had replied to her message. Her friend had told her she was dropping by, but had neglected to add when.

On TV, some breaking news bulletin was being aired, and when the word 'Millions' flashed by on the crawler, Vesta's attention was immediately drawn.

"Today a painting by Vincent Van Gogh was sold at auction for no less than three hundred million dollars!" an excitable newscaster intoned breathlessly.

"Three hundred million!" Vesta cried, suddenly feeling just as breathless as the woman on the screen. "For that ugly piece of crap? How is that even possible!"

Grace must have thought the exact same thing, for she gurgled, "Brap!"

"Brap indeed," said Vesta, rubbing her great-grandchild's back. "Did you hear that, sweetie? That ugly painting just sold for three hundred million smackeroos!"

"Mackemoos!" Grace prattled happily.

"Exactly!"

Just then, Scarlett walked in through the kitchen door, as was her habit. She was dressed to impress, in a short-short skirt and skimpy tank top, that emphasized her ample assets, her lips and nails a vivid red, as was her hair. It was hard to believe that she was the same age as Vesta herself, though it did take her some effort to look that way. "Hey, hun. Hey there, cutie pie," she said as she tickled Grace on the cheek with one of those long nails. "Everything all right, Vesta? You look like you've just seen a ghost."

"Some ugly-ass painting by some guy named Van Gauche just sold for no less than three hundred million bucks! I mean, my cats can paint better than this guy!"

"Which is exactly why you should join me and Marge for art class."

"What art class? What are you talking about?"

"Haven't I told you? I've been going to art class with Marge and Charlene."

She would have told her friend that art was for suckers, which was her standard response when someone asked her to do something she didn't want to, but she still had one eye on the screen, and that news ticker was still screaming.

"And I have to say that your daughter has a lot of talent, hun."

"You're kidding."

"Cross my heart. That girl is going places. Even Chanda is saying it."

"Chanda?"

"Chanda Chekhov. Our teacher."

"Huh. Well how about that?"

"Here, let me show you what I did last night," said Scarlett, and took out her phone. How she managed with those insane nails, Vesta did not know, but moments later she was staring at a drawing, and it wasn't half bad either.

She squinted as she took in her friend's creation. "Is that... a naked dude?"

"Yeah, we've been drawing nudes all month."

She reeled a little. "Wait a minute. Are you telling me that some naked guy comes in and you make drawings of him while he just... lies there on a couch?"

Scarlett grinned. "Pretty cool, huh? And I gotta tell you, ever since Naked Guy has started coming in, the number of students has tripled. And it's not all women either. We've got at least three guys in our class, though I think they're all gays."

"And is Marge drawing this guy, too?"

"Sure. We all are. Here, I took a picture of Marge's drawing."

Vesta stared at the sketch. Marge's work certainly showed a predilection for the artistic. Still, there was something wrong with the drawing, though she couldn't immediately put her finger on it. But then she had it. "Naked Guy is certainly well-endowed."

"Yeah, that's entirely Marge's personal interpretation. She's still struggling to get the anatomically correct proportions down on canvas."

Vesta quirked a quizzical brow. "The anatomically correct proportions?"

Scarlett grinned. "We all see what we want to see, Vesta."

She frowned. "I don't know if I like what my daughter is seeing. She is a married woman, you know. So frankly I think this is a little worrying." For a moment she stood there, rocking Grace, then finally she said, "I'm in."

"You're in?"

"Absolutely. Between this guy Van Gauche netting himself a cool three hundred million and Marge putting her marriage in serious jeopardy, it's a no-brainer."

"Yesss!" said Scarlet, and pumped the air with her fist.

"Mind you, my interest is strictly artistic, not to mention altruistic."

"Oh, for sure," said Scarlett, flashing her a cheeky grin.

"I'm doing it for Grace," Vesta explained. "If I can leave three hundred million bucks to my family, I will die a happy woman, knowing they're well taken care of."

"Absolutely," said Scarlett virtuously. "We're all doing it for Grace. Isn't that right, sweetie?" And she fondly kissed her godchild's pink chubby cheek.

"Beebie!" Grace babbled.

"And let's not forget about Marge," Vesta added. "My daughter has obviously developed some kind of unhealthy obsession with Naked Guy's package and needs to be saved from herself. Good thing she has a mother who cares."

"Bears!" Grace gurgled, always needing to have the last word.

CHAPTER 9

Tex had been expounding on his wife's penchant for fine arts for the past ten minutes, when Ida Baumgartner, the patient who'd sat quietly listening, suddenly piped up, "The thing is, doctor, that your wife may very well be a wonderful artist, but from what I hear, there is a very good reason why that may be the case."

Ida was Tex's most loyal and faithful patient. The bluff, apple-cheeked middle-aged lady came in at least once a week, with some real or perceived complaint, and was as garrulous as they came. Which is why it surprised him that she'd waited until now to interrupt his monologue.

"What do you mean?" he asked.

Ida pursed her lips censoriously. "You know how I hate to gossip, doctor. But I'm afraid Marge's art class isn't above reproach. *Morally* speaking, that is."

She placed particular emphasis on the word 'morally,' indicating it was of the utmost importance to her, as well it might be. Ida was a widow, but even when Mr. Baumgartner was still alive, she'd been at the forefront of the moral revolution in Hampton Cove, always seated in the first pew in St.

John's Church on Sunday morning, and first to decry the slackening of morals in their small town.

"What do you mean, morally speaking?" he asked, thoroughly befuddled.

She took a firmer grip on her purse, as if afraid Tex might make a grab for it when he heard what she had to say. "There is a persistent rumor floating around town that Chanda Chekhov uses male models to pose for his students." She gave a meaningful nod of the head and fixed him with a meaningful stare. "*Nude* male models!"

Tex opened his mouth to speak, but no words formed, so he hitched up the mandible. Nude male models? Posing for his wife? Now that was something she hadn't told him. Even though she had spoken at length about her artistic experience, the words nude, male or model had never passed her lips.

"Are you sure about this?" he finally asked. It was a rhetorical question, for Ida was always sure about any of the claims she made.

She now nodded significantly. "Oh, yes, I am."

He swallowed a little convulsively. "You mean there are males... in the nude?"

Once more she nodded slowly, a pair of glittering eyes fixed on him, allowing the meaning of her words to fully penetrate.

"So... a nude male model has been prancing around in front of my wife?"

"And for the full hour, too. A roomful of women, slavering over a naked man, studying him from every angle, under a row of spotlights. And people wonder why the divorce rates in this country are going through the roof. If it were up to me, this kind of sickening exhibition would be outlawed, and the perpetrator sentenced to life imprisonment for destroying the moral fiber of the community."

"I find this very hard to believe, Ida," he admitted.

"Oh, but I have it from someone who was there. She was so shocked at the spectacle that it took her a full week to recover. She also told me that attendance figures have tripled in the short time this man's services have been retained."

"You wouldn't happen to know this male model's name?"

"I didn't catch his name, but I know he's an artist himself. As one would expect." She adopted an expression of disgust. "Seedy bunch, one and all."

"Young?" he asked in a croaky voice.

"Twenty-four."

"Twenty-four-year-old artist," he murmured. "Naked in front of my wife."

"And Charlene Butterwick, your brother-in-law's *unmarried* partner."

"I had no idea," he confessed. It was probably a bad idea to show this chink in his armor in front of a patient, but he couldn't help it. The shock was too great.

"If I were you, Tex, I'd take a firm line with Marge," Ida advised.

"What do you mean?"

"Forbid her to go to this feast of immorality! This cornucopia of sin!"

"But it's her art, Ida. Her art!" His voice had taken on a bleating quality.

"I know. That's always their excuse. But at some point a man has to put his foot down. If this is allowed to go on, who knows what will happen next."

"Yes, I see what you mean."

"I wouldn't give a dime for that marriage of yours, which is exactly what these people want. These... libertines! So you just tell that wife of yours no more art classes," said Ida, summing up her point succinctly. "Or else."

"Or else what?" he asked, suddenly prey to indecisiveness.

"That's for you to decide, doctor," said Ida primly. "Far be it from me to poke around in your marriage." She said it with a straight face, even though poking around in other people's marriages was all she did, and did well. In fact if a degree would exist at colleges and universities for Pokology, Ida would take first prize.

"Well, thanks for warning me about this, Ida," he said. "I had no idea."

She reluctantly got up, then planted her hands on Tex's desk. "This is the way I see it. If my Burt had ever frequented some 'art' class where naked women pranced around all night, I'd have told him what was what so fast his head would have spun. No marriage can sustain this level of temptation, not even a great marriage like yours." She stood erect, and nodded with satisfaction, her work done. "And that's all I have to say about the matter. The rest is up to you."

After she had left, for a long time Tex just sat there, dark thoughts swirling in his mind, such as it was, creating then discarding wild schemes to save his marriage, which was obviously in grave danger from these artist people.

It took some time, but from the hard mental work an idea was born, so brilliant in its simplicity it took his breath away. And as he picked up the phone, he was actually smiling to himself, knowing that it was the only course of action open to him. The only course of action any concerned husband could take.

CHAPTER 10

That evening we were all enjoying a nice evening in—though of course almost all of our evenings are evenings in—when a call came that, judging from the look on Odelia's face, seemed more or less urgent and of a decidedly serious nature.

"Is it an art gallery?" asked Harriet excitedly. "Have they seen my painting and are they going to offer me an exhibition?"

"It's probably the supermarket," said Brutus, "telling Odelia that the cat food you ate is being recalled."

"Haha," I said. "Very funny, Brutus."

"No, but I'm actually serious for once," said Brutus. "It happens all the time, you know, that these big brands are forced to do a recall. Last week they had to recall an entire shipment of baby food, which turned out to contain arsenic."

This time I gulped, for I had indeed heard similar rumors in the past. So was it now our turn to become the victims of the mysterious phenomenon of perfectly good food turning out not to be as safe as advertised?

But then Odelia said, "We'll be there in five minutes, Uncle Alec," and hung up.

I sighed with relief. Clearly it wasn't the supermarket, unless Uncle Alec had lost his job and was temping there now.

"There's been a burglary," Odelia explained to Chase, who'd been watching a movie about World War II. The war quickly lost its appeal when the topic of a burglary came up, and he switched off the television and got up from the couch.

"Hey, I was watching that," said Dooley plaintively. "Now I'll never know who won the war."

"Where?" asked Chase curtly, all business all of a sudden.

"Tucker Street," said Odelia, then frowned. "Isn't that where Jay and Laia live?"

"Let's go," said Chase, already on his way out the door.

"Now that's a dedicated cop for you," said Brutus proudly. "Even when spending a nice evening with his family he can't wait to catch the bad guys."

Grace, who'd been gurgling happily, now gurgled some more, reminding Odelia and Chase that they might be ardent investigators, but they were also parents, which came with certain responsibilities, like taking care of their kid.

"We'll take her along with us," said Odelia after a moment's hesitation, and so it was a full contingent of Kingsleys that filed into Chase's pickup, which is a lot nicer than Odelia's. Of course it's not his pickup, per se, since it belongs to the police department, and in that sense actually to the people of Hampton Cove.

"Maybe we should buy a new car," Odelia now said as she held Grace on her lap, which probably isn't the right way to travel with a child in a car. "A family car, you know. Like a Volvo, maybe?"

"A Volvo!" Chase cried, aghast at the mere mention of the V word.

"You know what I mean. A car where we can install a safety seat for Grace."

"We can put her in the back," Chase suggested.

Odelia glanced over her shoulder, through the steel mesh partition that was put in place to keep violent prisoners from attacking the driver, and shook her head. "I don't think so, babe."

Us cats, of course, didn't have the benefit of such careful consideration, since all four of us were in the spot usually reserved for the bad guys that habitually ride in the back of Chase's squad car after having been arrested for their crime.

At least we didn't have to wear handcuffs.

"It doesn't have to be a Volvo," Odelia continued. "It could be a minivan."

"A minivan!" Chase cried, as he took a firmer grip on the steering wheel.

"I mean, I love my old pickup, but maybe it's time to trade it in."

Grace must have sensed she was the topic of conversation, for she said, "Brmljgup," and released a trail of drool that slid down her mom's front.

"She has a funny way of communicating," Brutus remarked.

"Yes, she does," said Harriet. "Do all infants drool so much, Max?"

She seemed to think I was the expert on human infants. "I have no idea."

"I think they do," said Brutus. "At least the ones I've seen all have a problem keeping their saliva in their mouths."

"I think it's because they don't have teeth," said Dooley. "I saw a documentary once and it said that young humans are born without teeth, and that it takes months before they get them, and once they do, they lose them again, and then it takes years before they get their final ones. It's all very complicated."

"It's no different for cats," I said. "Kittens are also born without teeth. Only it doesn't take months but weeks before they get them, and months before they get their permanent teeth."

"Sounds like cats are a lot quicker off the mark," said Brutus proudly.

"Well, I hope Grace gets her teeth soon," said Harriet, "cause last night she drooled all over me. And the worst part was that I didn't even notice until it was too late. I was practically standing in a puddle!"

It seemed to me that Harriet was slightly exaggerating, but I refrained from comment. After all, what did I know? Like I said, I'm not a baby expert. To me these small humans are very strange, and their behavior most puzzling.

We had finally arrived, and Chase parked behind a fellow officer's squad car. Tucker Street used to be located in a bad part of town, but has been gentrifying, with many houses being torn down, and others being turned into apartments and lofts, all of them now available at a hefty premium, as is often the case.

The street itself had been partly excavated, and signs everywhere announced that 'Tucker Street says NO to cobblestone!' Or even 'Cobblestone? NEVER!'

"What's a cobblestone, Max?" asked Dooley, who had noticed the same thing.

"They're a square sort of granite stone," I said, "used to pave the streets."

"They're very inconvenient for cyclists," said Harriet knowingly, as if she drove her bicycle up and down cobblestone streets all day long.

We all got out and picked our way across the excavated street to the scene of the action: several police officers stood milling about, shooting the breeze, and then we spotted Uncle Alec, who came walking up to us, wiping his brow, as if all the cares of the world were resting on his burly shoulders, as oftentimes they did.

"Why all the uniforms?" asked Chase. "Did the burglar get away?"

"Worse," said the Chief as he pointed in the direction of a man who sat crouched next to what looked like a body. "He's dead."

"How did that happen?"

"He broke into one of those upstairs apartments," said the Chief, pointing to the house in front of which the dead person was lying, "but as he was leaving he must have slipped and fallen and broken his neck. Or at least that's what I think happened. I'm waiting for Abe to confirm."

Abe is Abe Cornwall, the county coroner, and the man who's called upon in situations like these to determine if a person is dead, and if so, what made them that way.

We walked up to the coroner as he worked his magic, and as he got up, with a distinct creaking of the knees, he scratched his scalp, from which an abundance of electric gray hair sprouted. "Well, looks like you've got yourself a dead one, Alec."

"Yeah, I knew that already, Abe," said Uncle Alec. "But did he fall or what?"

"That is certainly what it looks like. Dead on impact, I'd say."

"Christ," said the Chief as he gazed up at the windows of the house.

"Do we know what apartment he broke into?" asked Odelia.

"Yeah, one Jay Green," said the Chief.

Odelia gasped, even as she rocked Grace in her arms.

She'd turned the kid's face away, so she didn't have to see the unhappy burglar who met such a sad fate.

"That's the couple I've been helping," she said.

"Helping with what?" asked her uncle.

Ever since Odelia had her baby, her uncle hasn't been all that keen on her working as a police consultant anymore, on account of the fact that he feels that a young mother shouldn't put herself in danger. But of course Odelia being Odelia, she went right back to work the moment she could.

"Jay and his fiancée Laia are the victims of what looks like a harassment campaign by a stalker, and they've asked me to find out who's behind it."

"And? Who is behind it?"

"I've only just started to investigate, Uncle Alec."

"Could be this guy right here," he said, pointing to the dead burglar.

Just then, Laia came walking up to us, looking distinctly distressed.

"Oh, God," she said. "One of the neighbors called us and told me that our loft had been broken into. We came home as soon as we could."

"You were out?" asked the Chief a little gruffly, as if the girl was personally to blame for this burglary.

"Yeah, we were at the cinema," said Laia, nodding. She glanced briefly at the man at her feet, then asked, in a tremulous sort of voice, "Is that... him?"

"I'm afraid it is," said Odelia, her voice exuding a lot more warmth and sympathy than her uncle's.

"Is he... dead?"

No one replied, since it was pretty obvious what the answer was. Instead, Uncle Alec said, "Would you say that anything was stolen, Miss..."

"Twine. Laia Twine."

The Chief frowned. "Twine as in Algis Twine? The gambling king?"

Laia nodded with a touch of embarrassment. "He's my dad."

A window had opened upstairs, and Jay's face appeared. "Sweetie—your necklace. It's gone!"

"Oh, no!" said Laia, clutching a distraught hand to her neck. "Not my necklace!"

"What necklace is this?" asked Odelia.

"It's a necklace I got from my mother. It's worth a small fortune."

"Are you sure it's missing!" Uncle Alec shouted to the man upstairs.

"Yeah, I can't find it anywhere!" Jay shouted back.

Uncle Alec grumbled something under his breath, then stomped in the direction of the door. "This is no way to conduct an investigation," we could hear him mutter, and then he disappeared inside, ready to take Jay's statement in connection with Laia's priceless necklace.

I saw that Laia was staring down at the body of the burglar again, who lay face down on the gravel. "He must have taken it," she said, her face white as a sheet.

Chase must have noticed the same phenomenon, for he quickly took her by the arm and led her away. "Let's go inside, Miss Twine," he said courteously.

"When... when can I have my necklace back?" she asked, as she staggered a little, leaning heavily on Chase's arm now.

"As soon as the investigation is done," Chase assured her.

"If Mommy finds out, she'll kill me," said Laia, and disappeared inside with Chase.

"Well, I guess that's just about enough excitement for one evening," said Abe as he stretched his weary form. He then told his people to wrap up the body and take it to the coroner's office.

"When can Laia have her necklace back?" asked Odelia.

"Soon," said Abe, looking a little distracted.

"You look tired, Abe," said Odelia commiseratively.

"You wouldn't believe my workload right now," said the coroner. "My fridges are overflowing with stiffs. It's as if they all made a pact to die in the same week." Then he smiled at Odelia and poked a tender finger in Grace's cheek. The kid took hold of the man's frizzy hair and studied it, then giggled happily.

"She probably thinks it's cotton candy," said Odelia.

"Maybe it is!" said the coroner gamely.

Grace certainly enjoyed the moment, until she yanked at the man's hair, hard, and he let out a yelp of pain. Looks like it wasn't cotton candy after all.

"I'll send my report to your uncle as soon as I can, all right?" he said, his mood slightly less exuberant. I guess nobody likes their hair being yanked, no matter how cute the perpetrator. And then he grabbed his coroner's bag and was off, presumably working through the night to get on top of his workload.

"Better him than me," said Odelia as she stared after the man.

"I don't like that guy," said Dooley. "He always smells funny."

"That's because he works with dead people all the time," said Brutus with a slight grin. "He cuts them open and he removes their heart and liver and stomach and intestines and uses a buzz saw to drill a hole in their skull so he can scoop out their brains. And of course that kind of thing leaves a stench." He brought his face close to Dooley's. "The stench of death!" he added with a sort of ghoulish delight.

Dooley shivered. "Crikey!"

"Don't worry, Dooley," said Harriet with a reproachful look at her boyfriend. "I'm sure he washes his hands each

NIC SAINT

time he cuts open a dead body." She glanced up at Odelia. "So what are we still doing here? We know who stole the necklace. It was the dead guy who face-planted on the sidewalk. Mystery solved. Let's go."

"Not so fast," said Odelia. "There's a story here," she explained. "A big story. I can smell it." And then she, too, disappeared inside the apartment, presumably to get some more background information on the burglary.

Dooley stuck his nose in the air and sniffed. "I don't smell anything," he said.

"Which is probably a good thing," I said. Like Harriet, I was ready to go home.

CHAPTER 11

Vesta had to admit this art class was absolutely her thing. There were plenty of friends and acquaintances present. People like Scarlett, of course, her best friend, but also Marge, and then there was Charlene Butterwick, practically her daughter-in-law, Vena Aleman, the vet, Blanche Captor, Dolores Peltz, Sarah Flunk, Bambi Wiggins, their mailwoman. Even Marcie Trapper was there, their neighbor. It was almost a who's who of everyone who was anyone in Hampton Cove.

"Very cozy," she told the man who was seated next to her. He was, in fact, the only male in attendance, apart from Chanda Chekhov, the teacher, a whiskered fella with lots of hair and a sort of laidback approach to the creation of art.

"Yes, it's one of my favorite art classes," the man returned politely.

His name was Gallagher Davenport, and he looked as much like an artist as any artist Vesta had ever seen: dressed in a sort of snazzy orange coat with frilly lace trimmings, and a green felt hat on his head, in spite of the fact that temperatures inside were soaring, to say the least. Probably on account of the nude male model who was supposed to put in an appearance any second now. No one needs a nude male model with goosebumps. It detracts from the appeal.

"Art runs in the family," Vesta revealed, glad to find such a listening ear in this fellow artist. "My daughter is over there," she explained, waving to Marge, who didn't seem all that pleased with the presence of her mom for some reason. "And then of course my cat is an artist, as well."

When the guy regarded her a little strangely, she took out her phone and showed him a video she'd shot just that afternoon of Harriet and Brutus hard at work creating their own unique brand of art.

The man sat up with a jerk as he took her phone and regarded the video with the sort of attention to detail your true art lover likes to see.

"But this is amazing, my dear lady," he said finally. "And you say this is your cat?"

"Yeah, absolutely. That's Harriet," she explained, pointing to Harriet, who was standing on top of a chair giving directions. "And that's Brutus. He's doing the grunt work, and Harriet is guiding him. She's the real artist in the family, see."

"Absolutely amazing," the man murmured as he seemed entranced by the spectacle.

"Bob Ross is Harriet's personal favorite," Vesta prattled on. "Harriet can watch Bob Ross any time, day or night. She simply never tires of watching the guy. I believe she considers him her role model and her guiding light as an artist."

"It's very soothing to watch two cats creating art like this," her fellow student conceded. "Very soothing indeed."

"Oh, absolutely," said Vesta. "I watched them for half an hour this afternoon and I never had such a great nap."

The man suddenly turned to her. "Say, my dear lady, how much for the two of them?"

"What are you talking about?" she asked, unprepared for the sudden turn the conversation had taken.

"How much do you want for both cats? They are a pair, correct? One is the creative genius and the other the executor?"

"My cats aren't for sale, buddy," she said, and yanked her phone from the man's hands.

"I'll give you a hundred bucks for the both of them." And when she gave him a look of astonishment, he wrongly interpreted this as her driving a hard bargain, and quickly came back with, "Okay, two hundred bucks, but that's my final offer."

"Like I said, my cats are not for sale," she reiterated with a touch of frostiness, and shook her head at this mercantile streak in one whom she'd considered a fellow creative.

Gallagher Davenport opened his mouth to make one final comment—perhaps raising his offer even more—but Chanda now cleared his throat, desiring speech.

"I have an announcement to make," Chanda said. "I'm sorry to say that our model for the evening hasn't shown up." When loud cries of disappointment greeted his words, he hastened to add, "But I've arranged for a replacement. A man who has graciously agreed to fill in the void that our handsome young friend has left by his absence." He now turned to the door, through which a man came walking, dressed in a dressing gown. "Fellow art lovers, please welcome... Tex!"

And much to Vesta's astonishment, her own son-in-law stepped to the fore!

"Tex, what are you doing here!" Marge cried.

Tex, whose face had taken on the color of a ripe plum, swallowed once or twice, and said, with as much dignity as he could muster, "I'm here to model."

"But..."

"Please take your position on the stage, Mr. Poole," said

Chanda, pointing to the small dais in front of the class. "And drop the robe."

Tex hesitated, but then finally dropped the robe, revealing a puny hairless chest and a snazzy-looking pair of pink boxers with tiny blue stethoscopes.

The art teacher regarded the boxers with a sort of astonished surmise, and gestured for Tex to drop that final garment as well. But Tex, stubbornly refusing, draped himself across the divan that had been set up, and struck a pose.

Chanda, shaking his head at this lack of artistic finesse, decided to leave the doctor be, and said, "Ladies and gentleman. Pick up your pencils and... go!"

Vesta locked eyes with the good doctor for a moment, and the man's color deepened even more, if that was possible. Then he looked away, the blush of shame that had mantled his cheeks quickly spreading along his neck and chest, until he looked the victim of some dangerous disease.

Good thing they were obliged to draw in black and white, Vesta thought, or the result of today's class would have been a study in scarlet.

CHAPTER 12

*A*rt class had finished by the time we got home from our trip into town, and something very disturbing must have happened, for Marge and Tex weren't on speaking terms. Marge had stormed into the house, followed by a disconsolate-looking Tex, though judging from Gran's smiling face whatever drama had befallen our family, it couldn't be all bad, for she was grinning from ear to ear.

"What's going on?" asked Odelia when Gran breezed in for a little chat.

"You'll never guess," said the old lady.

"It's bad, isn't it?" asked Odelia. "I just saw Mom's face and it spelled storm."

"She should be proud. Your dad has launched himself in a new and promising career."

"What career?" asked Odelia, clearly as puzzled as the rest of us.

"He's a male model now."

And as she spoke these words, she burst into a torrent of laughter.

Odelia wasn't laughing, and neither was Chase. "A male what?" he asked.

"A male model. The regular model was a no-show, and so the teacher introduced a replacement. Imagine our surprise when it turned out to be Tex!"

"But why?"

"How should I know what goes on in that man's head?" She shook her own head. "I've always said that these medical men have too much brain in those heads of theirs, and sooner or later something has to give. Looks like your dad has finally gone over the edge and is now in cloud cuckoo land."

And with these words, she abruptly left, clearly eager to have a first-row seat to the drama that was unfolding next door.

"My dad, a model," said Odelia, still shocked.

"I don't believe it," said Chase. "Your gran must have misunderstood."

"Yeah, obviously. Why would my dad suddenly want to be a model?"

But since no more explanations seemed forthcoming, we decided it was time to leave for cat choir. After all, the affairs of humans are all very fascinating, but at some point they have to take a back seat to the affairs of cats, our first priority.

And so the four of us headed out, traipsing along the sidewalk, wondering what had induced Odelia's dad to change careers all of a sudden.

"He probably needs the extra money," said Harriet. "Life is getting more and more expensive, as we all know, and Tex must have decided to take a second job."

"I don't think being a male model pays the big bucks," I said.

"No, but it does," said Harriet. "Everyone knows that a

model has to start somewhere, and probably Tex is trying to break into the big leagues by taking it one step at a time." A sort of dreamy look had stolen over her face. "Soon he'll be walking the catwalk in Paris, London, Milan and New York for Fashion Week. I'm sure he'll be one of the most-sought after male models of our time, and then, who knows, maybe he could even break into the movie business and become an actor."

"Tex is too old to be a model or an actor," said Brutus.

"No, he's not. The industry needs models of all ages," said Harriet. "And besides, I think Tex still looks pretty good for his age, don't you?"

Brutus chose to wisely keep his tongue.

I didn't think Tex had the right look or the right age to launch himself as a top model either, but then I wasn't really interested in that side of the man's career.

At least, I wasn't until Dooley made a remark that set me thinking.

"If Tex drops his job as a doctor, who's going to pay the bills?" he asked. "And if no one is paying the bills, who's going to buy us food and litter?"

"Oh, dear," I said. Dooley was right, of course. Since it's very hard for cats to hold down a job, we depend on our humans to keep us in the style to which we've become accustomed. "I hope Tex isn't foolish enough to drop his job as a doctor."

"Haven't you listened to a word I said?" said Harriet. "Tex is going to hit the big time, I'm sure of it. Before you know it he'll be on the cover of *Vogue*. And let me tell you, those models make more money than a measly small-town doctor."

Somehow I didn't think this was so, and even if it was, the chances of Tex becoming a top model and being on the cover of *Vogue* were slim to none.

"Isn't *Vogue* for women only?" Brutus ventured.

"I'm sure they'll make an exception for an exceptional talent," Harriet said.

And as the discussion raged on, suddenly I thought I heard something behind us. When I glanced back, I distinctly saw movement. Someone or something furtively ducking into the bushes lining the sidewalk, moving out of sight.

Odd, I thought. But when I tried to bring this to the attention of my friends, they were too busy discussing Tex's future prospects—or lack thereof—to bother.

And as we finally reached the park, I had this strong sense of foreboding, and when I glanced back once more, I clearly saw a flash. And this time I was more certain than ever: it was the light of a streetlamp reflecting on a smartphone.

Someone was filming us!

CHAPTER 13

"Honey, what were you thinking!"

"I was thinking about you, with that naked model artist guy," said Tex miserably as he carefully folded his pants and draped them over the back of a chair.

They were in their bedroom, where no prying eyes or inquisitive voices could interrupt them. Marge was washing her face with a special lotion preparatory to applying the even more special—and costly—cream she'd recently bought on Scarlett Canyon's instigation. A cream designed to keep her looking young forever, if the commercials were to be believed. And even though by all rights she should be mad at her husband, thinking back to the moment he'd been lying there, in those ridiculous pink boxers, once again brought a smile to her face.

"At least you could have worn a decent pair of boxers," she now said.

"I had no idea I was actually going to have to be a model!" Tex cried, sitting down on the bed, bouncing down once, then bouncing up again, too wired to sit still for even one second. "All I wanted was to talk to your teacher. Tell him to switch from live model drawing to still lifes. But the moment I arrived he seemed to think I was volunteering as a model, and before I knew what was going on, he had me in a dressing gown and mounting that stage!"

"I thought you'd managed for the other guy not to show up."

"I had nothing to do with that. And Chekhov didn't seem to know either."

Marge laughed her tinkling laugh. "You should have told Chanda you're a doctor, not a model."

"I did tell him. More than once. But I don't think he heard."

"He was probably glad to have someone—*anyone* to model for us."

"I can't believe he actually made me go through with that," Tex grumbled.

"And I can't believe you agreed to go through with it," said Marge. She smiled at her hubby of twenty-five years. "Though I have to say you still have what it takes, honey. You were a big hit."

"I don't care. This was the first and last time I'm doing something like this."

"Are you sure? You could turn this into a career. Quit medicine and go into modeling full-time."

"Never!" he cried, aghast at her suggestion.

"So you're just going to let this other guy model in the nude for your wife again?" she asked. A spasm of unease galvanized his lanky frame and he grimaced. "Are you sure you won't get jealous again and storm in there to drag me out?"

"Now you're just teasing me," he complained.

"Of course I'm teasing you! Though I have to say I appreciate you standing up to protect my virtue, honey."

"When Ida told me the story about this guy I had to do something," he said with a shrug, then eyed her curiously. "So you thought I looked all right out there?"

"You looked absolutely fine," she said, and meant it, too.

He might not have the chiseled chest and sculpted musculature of the other guy, but Tex still looked pretty good for his age. He'd obviously been taking good care of himself. And besides, he looked like a real person, whereas the other guy looked like something out of a magazine, photoshopped and unreal.

"Just promise me next time you'll change your boxers," she repeated.

"There will be no next time," he grumbled.

"So you say," she said, and gave him a light pat on those boxers—the same ones he'd worn in class. Somehow she had a feeling those boxers would be the talk of the town tomorrow. She got up, ready to turn in. "Let's go to bed, mh?"

He gave her a lopsided grin. "Want me to do some private modeling for you?"

"Oh, yes, please, Doctor Poole," she said virtuously.

Half an hour later a knock sounded at the door.

"Is everything all right in there?" the voice of her mother sounded behind the door. "You two haven't killed each other, have you?"

She smiled at her husband, who gave her a wolfish grin in return.

"No, we're fine," she yelled back. "In fact we're better than fine!"

Who knew that some light male modeling would prove such a boon for their love life? Something to mention to Odelia. She could write about it for the women's section of the *Gazette* tomorrow. Without naming names, of course.

But then Tex got his second wind, and she forgot all about their daughter.

Ma must have been listening, for she could hear her mumble, "Get a room."

CHAPTER 14

The next morning we were all present and accounted for in Uncle Alec's office. And when I say all, I mean myself, Dooley, Chase and Odelia, and of course the big man himself.

The latter had a few things to discuss with our intrepid detectives, namely the unfortunate demise of one Dylon Pipe, burglar by profession, but apparently not a very good one, or else he wouldn't have toppled to his death outside the apartment building he was burgling.

"No coroner's report yet," the Chief said as he glared at me, as if I'd personally prevented the coroner from doing his job. "Abe told me he's got a backlog of bodies to process, so it might be a couple of days before he gets round to our friendly neighborhood burglar. But so far it looks like an accidental death."

"Any news on that necklace?" asked Odelia. "Only Laia called me this morning, all atwitter about her necklace. Apparently it's worth a great deal of money."

"How much is a great deal?" asked Uncle Alec.

"Let's just say it could buy you a house... or ten," said Odelia.

The Chief's eyebrows shot up. "Ten houses? And they kept that thing at the loft?"

"She only just got it as a present from her mom and dad," Odelia explained, "so they hadn't decided where to keep it yet."

"In a safe at the bank would be my best bet," said Chase.

"Well, I'm sure they will put it there now, once they get it back." She shot her uncle a meaningful look, but the latter merely shook his head.

"I'm sorry, but Abe says Mr. Pipe didn't have the necklace on him. In fact nothing of value was found on the body, I'm afraid."

"But how is that possible?" asked Odelia.

"Maybe it fell out of his pocket and someone picked it up?" Chase suggested.

"It's possible," Uncle Alec conceded. "At any rate, I've got a couple of uniforms doing a house-to-house to see if anyone saw anything suspicious last night."

"Could be that one of the neighbors saw the guy take a tumble and picked up the necklace," said Chase. "Or a passerby, figuring it was their lucky night."

"We'll know more when I get the report from the neighborhood canvass," said Odelia's uncle. "Though from what I hear that neighborhood isn't extremely cooperative. Seems they're up in arms against these street works. Something about the cobblestones. They even formed an anti-cobblestone committee."

"What do they have against cobblestone?" asked Chase, genuinely curious.

"Something to do with it being bad for their cars," said the Chief. "And making too much noise when someone drives through the street."

"It's true that a cobblestone street makes a lot more noise than an asphalted one," said Odelia. "I once wrote an article about it for the paper, with an expert measuring the decibels produced by the two types. There's a marked difference."

"I thought the whole point of a cobblestone street was to reduce traffic, and lower the speed," said Chase, "since driving across those stones makes drivers automatically slow down."

"Yeah, well, they're dead set against it," said the Chief. "In other news," he said, changing the topic from one he clearly wasn't all that interested in, "did you know that Dylon Pipe and his victim knew each other?" He directed this question at his niece, whom he considered an expert on all things Jay Green through her recent association with the guy.

"Jay and Dylon knew each other?" asked Odelia, sounding surprised.

"Yeah, they were in school together. They're the same age, in fact, and still move in the same circles. The art world," he added for Chase's sake.

"Dylon was also an artist?" asked Odelia.

"He was. And a popular model at the art school. Evening classes." He leaned back with a grin on his broad face. "And guess who's one of the students in his class?"

"Mom and Gran," said Odelia.

Uncle Alec frowned. "Sounds like you know more about it than me."

"Oh, and Scarlett has been going, too," said Odelia. "And Charlene, of course."

Her uncle's frown deepened. "Charlene and Dylon Pipe? She didn't tell me."

"It's just drawing, Uncle Alec. Nothing more."

"Mh," he said, clearly not convinced that nothing untoward was going on. "Anyway, he's dead now," he added, miraculously cheering up a great deal. "And when he failed to show up for his class last night, the teacher came up with a last-minute replacement. A man we all know and love." And with a sort of flourish, he turned his computer screen, where the picture of a naked man was featured.

Though when I looked closer, I saw that the man was actually wearing a pair of pink boxers to cover his modesty. It was Odelia's dad, of course.

"I heard the story, but I hadn't seen the pictures," said Chase. He suppressed a grin, darting curious glances at his wife, whose face had turned beet-red.

"I did not have to see that," said our human. "I so did not have to see that."

"Same here," said the Chief. "But unfortunately I had no choice in the matter. This picture is circulating on all social media this morning. In fact it's the talk of the town. And the precinct, of course." He growled, "And because this is my brother-in-law making a total ass of himself, they all figure I should be the first one to see any new pictures or memes as they appear online."

"Someone took a lot of pictures," said Chase, snickering freely now as his boss scrolled through some more images of what must have been a historic session.

Odelia averted her gaze. "My eyes," she said plaintively. "They're burning!"

CHAPTER 15

Odelia was back at her office. The meeting with her uncle hadn't gone as she had anticipated. For one thing, she still couldn't give Laia Twine good news about her necklace, poor girl. And now they even had to learn the shocking news that the man who had stolen their necklace was actually a friend of Jay's, the poor guy.

Dylon Pipe must really have been down on his luck, to go and burgle his friend's place. He must have discovered that Jay was dating a rich young woman, and must have figured he wanted some of that for himself.

She was pretty sure the necklace would eventually be found, though. Maybe it had slipped underneath a car parked nearby, or fallen into a crack or even slipped through a sewer grate when Dylon hit the ground. She had every faith in her uncle's people, who were doing their utmost to find the young burglar's loot.

She glanced over to her cats, sound asleep in a corner of her office, and smiled. They, too, had had to brave the sight of her dad in those ridiculous boxers, but apparently they had endured the experience with admirable fortitude, as had she.

No girl likes to see her daddy, who will always be something of a personal hero to her, making a fool of himself like that. And she'd just picked up the phone to call her mom when a man walked into her office who she'd never seen before.

He looked like a dandy, with a long velvet coat and a green felt hat on his head.

"I greet you, Mrs. Kingsley," said the man, speaking in formal tones, a supercilious expression plastered all over an elongated face. "My name is Gallagher Davenport, and I have an interesting business proposition for you."

"A business proposition?" she asked, sitting back as she studied the guy.

"Your grandmother, Vesta Muffin, is a fellow art student. We met last night in art class," he said, taking a seat, "and she showed me an intriguing video of her cats, Harriet and Brutus, engaged in the creation of their art."

"Oh, that's right," she said. "I saw that."

"I thought it was the most amazing thing I've ever seen," said the man, darting a curious glance to Max and Dooley, who had woken up the moment the man entered, and were listening intently, since the conversation had turned to a topic that was clearly of interest to them.

"Yeah, it is pretty amazing," she agreed. She was even thinking of putting the video on the *Gazette* website, figuring it would attract a lot of eyeballs to the site.

"The thing is, I offered your grandmother a great deal of money to take those two cats off her hands, but she turned me down. It was only later that I discovered Harriet and Brutus aren't actually her cats, and that the real owner is you, Mrs. Kingsley." He inclined his head deferentially in Odelia's direction.

"Well, let's just say the cats are co-owned by the whole family," said Odelia. "Me, my mom and my grandmother."

"That's very gratifying to hear," said the guy, looking well pleased. "Which is why I'm going to make you the same offer I made Mrs. Muffin. Two hundred dollars for both cats."

Odelia eyed the man curiously. She had to admit she was intrigued. "Why do you want to buy my cats, Mr. Davenport?"

"Why, to make them famous, of course. Never since Bob Ross has the world seen such a thing. Just the mere sight of Harriet and Brutus engaged in their art... Let's just say it has a distinctly soothing effect on a person. It nurtures the soul. It brings a smile to one's lips. And right now the world is in need of such a thing."

"So you think Harriet and Brutus might be the next Bob Ross?"

"Oh, I have no doubt about it. In fact they'll be bigger than Ross, since they combine the two things the internet loves: watching people paint, and being cats. Cats and painting, in other words, is the magic formula the world has been waiting for. You mark my words, it's going to be the next big thing. Bigger than the pimple popping challenge or even the Tide pods challenge." He must have felt he was giving the game away, for he quickly added, "With the caveat that a professional marketer puts his genius behind the endeavor, of course."

"Oh, so you're a professional marketer?"

"Indeed I am. Davenport & Sons is the company my father started many moons ago. We represent several of the Fortune 500 companies, but this," he said, pointing to Max and Dooley, "would be a personal project. A passion project, so to speak."

"Well, I hate to disappoint you, Mr. Davenport, for you do

sound very passionate about this, but I'm afraid Harriet and Brutus are not for sale."

She thought she could hear twin sighs of relief from Max and Dooley, but it was drowned out by the sigh of disappointment from the man in front of her.

"Three hundred," he said now, breathing a little stertorously and eyeing her intently through lowered lashes.

"Absolutely not."

He grimaced. "Five hundred, if you throw in that fat orange one over there and that skinny fluffball."

This time she distinctly heard Max gasp in shock, and say, "Hey, buddy, for your information I'm blorange, not orange!"

"And he's not fat, he's big-boned!" Dooley added for good measure.

"I'm afraid I can't accept your offer, Mr. Davenport," she said, giving the man a cold look. Insult my cats, and you insult me, she thought. "And now if you'll excuse me, I have work to do."

"I see," said the man, and slowly rose to his feet. Then he leaned over the desk and fixed her with a steely look. "One thousand dollars. Take it or leave it."

"I'll leave it, and so can you," she said, meeting his look and adding some frostiness to her own implacable stare.

He abruptly straightened, shook his head in distaste, and left her office without another word.

"Despicable man," she murmured.

"Thank you for not selling us to that man, Odelia," said Dooley.

"Yeah, I don't think I like him," Max added.

"I'd never sell you guys," she assured them.

And just as she was getting ready to return to her article about last night's burglary, the door opened once more and Davenport strode in again, walked straight up to her and showed her his phone for some reason.

"I took these pictures last night," he said. "I believe they're of your father."

She found herself looking at the now familiar pictures of her dad in his funny boxers. "Yes, so what?" she said, getting really sick and tired of this odious man.

"If you don't sell me your cats, I'll make sure these pictures are on every social media network, and your father will be the laughingstock of the town. I believe he's a doctor, so I assume he wouldn't want his reputation dragged through the mud?"

"My dad's pictures are already out there, buster," she said icily. "And now if you don't get out of my office, I'll have you thrown out, is that understood?"

He stood there, wavering for a moment, then stalked out and slammed the door.

"What a terrible man!" Dooley cried.

"I guess it comes with the job," said Odelia. As a reporter she'd met some really unpleasant people, but this guy definitely took the cake.

"I'm glad you kicked him out," said Max.

"Yeah, if you hadn't thrown him out, I would have bitten him in the patootie!" said Dooley, and showed her his teeth to prove he wasn't kidding.

In spite of the recent experience, she had to laugh.

"Thanks, Dooley. It's good to know you've got my back."

"Always!" said the fluffy gray cat fervently.

CHAPTER 16

Each time Odelia got stuck writing an article, she knew she could simply ask her boss Dan for his input. The man was probably as old as Methuselah and because of his advanced age, and his extensive experience, he knew pretty much everything there was to know about everyone in town, and a lot of others as well.

And so it was that she found herself in the editor's office, listening to his sage advice. Dan leaned back in his chair and steepled his fingers, his long white beard waggling as he chuckled amusedly. "Algis Twine. How about that? Do you know I wrote an article about that guy years ago? You'll find it in the archives under the C for Crook."

"So he's a crook, is he, Laia's dad?"

"I'm joking, of course," said Dan. "Algis isn't really a crook, in the sense that he made his fortune legally. Even though he didn't start out as a businessman, it's true that he did a great job building his empire. But if it hadn't been for his wife Matilda, he would probably be in jail right now. Or living in utter squalor."

"Tell me all, Dan," said Odelia with a smile, for she sensed that her editor was chomping at the bit to tell her a story.

"Once upon a time, Algis Twine was a lowlife thug, member of an extremist group that loved nothing better than to make trouble. They used to organize meetings and demonstrations, simply as an excuse to get into a fight with the police and bust some heads and crack some skulls. His nickname back then was The Bludgeoner, which tells you all you need to know about him. He was in and out of prison pretty much all through his teens, and it was only when he finally met a young IT student that he managed to turn his life around for the better."

"Let me guess. Matilda Twine was the IT student."

"Yeah, Matilda Scrape had this idea for a website that would facilitate something that didn't exist back then: online gambling. It was a novel idea, and one that probably no one thought would work. But Matilda and Algis persisted, and before long their site was the number-one gambling site in the country—for a long time the only site. Now we know, of course, that online gambling is as big a business as physical gambling in casinos and such, but back then it was something totally new and unheard of."

"It made them billionaires," said Odelia, jotting down the odd note. It would all serve as background information for the article she intended to write.

"Absolutely," said Dan. He'd taken a cigar from his drawer and now sniffed at it with relish, put it in his mouth, chewed on it for a moment, and returned it to his drawer, unsmoked. He was trying to stop, and this seemed as good a way as any.

"But why are they so dead set against Jay Green as a potential husband for their daughter?"

"Well, Jay doesn't have any money, and so he's not the kind of match they had in mind for their daughter."

"I talked to Bud Zuk, who was her boyfriend before she met Jay."

"Now the Zuks are more the kind of people the Twines want to be associated with. Rich and well-connected, so Bud would be the ideal husband for Laia."

"Do you think the Twines could be behind this stalking business?"

"Could be," said Dan with a shrug. "Though if they are, chances are they're not personally involved. They're much too clever for that."

"Laia and Jay just want it to stop," said Odelia. "And now with this burglary…" She thought for a moment. "Do you think Laia's parents are behind the burglary?"

"It could all be part of the same campaign, for sure," said Dan. "Only young Dylon Pipe turned out to be a lousy candidate for the job."

"I mean, someone must have told him about that necklace," said Odelia.

"Or it could be a coincidence," her boss suggested. "Sometimes burglars get lucky. Or unlucky, as in this case. Where did they keep the necklace? In a safe?"

"Laia kept it tucked away underneath a stack of underwear," said Odelia, and saw her boss wince at the thought of a multi-million-dollar gem lying in Laia's underwear drawer.

A knock sounded at the door, and when it opened, the familiar face of Laia appeared. The young woman looked even paler and drawn than the night before, and Odelia said, "Just go to my office and take a seat. I'll be there in a second."

Laia nodded and retreated, quietly closing the door.

Dan gave her a meaningful look. "Are you sure you can handle this case, honey? I mean, you're a mother now, so maybe you shouldn't mix with the sleazeballs of this world?"

She got up. "Don't you worry about me, Dan. I can handle myself."

"I know," he said, and actually looked relieved. For a while he'd been worried she would quit her job, but now that she was back, he could see she was more determined than ever to be the best reporter she could be. And a good thing, too.

CHAPTER 17

I have to say I was glad when Laia walked into the office. I was expecting that man Gallagher Davenport to return and try to snatch me and Dooley and put us to work as paw painters along with Harriet and Brutus. But instead it was Laia, giving us a shy smile, and then finally our human returned, the last defense against the cat snatchers of this world.

And so I relaxed again, and so did Dooley.

"Do you think Davenport will try to buy us again, Max?" asked Dooley.

"I don't know," I said. "Though he looks like the kind of guy who doesn't give up without a fight."

"Yeah, he had that determined look in his eyes," said Dooley.

"Determined and evil," I added.

"You think that man is evil?"

"Oh, absolutely. I mean, who calls a blorange big-boned cat like me an orange fatty?"

"And me a skinny fluffball," Dooley added with a touch of defiance.

Good thing Odelia was there to protect us.

"Odelia will never sell us, will she?" asked Dooley, still looking slightly worried about the prospect of being sold, like a football player or other sports star.

"Odelia will never sell us," I said, and I felt convinced that my words had the ring of absolute truth. "And neither will Gran or Marge."

"Good," said Dooley, and I could see the tension dissipating from his corpus and finally being able to relax again.

"So what brings you here?" asked Odelia, though I had a feeling she knew full well what brought the young lady to our doorstep once more.

"I talked to your uncle just now," said Laia, who was sitting at the edge of her chair, not as much at ease as Dooley and myself. Maybe she was afraid someone was going to buy her, too, and put her to work as a YouTube painter.

"What did he say?" asked Odelia.

"His people have talked to all of our neighbors, and so far no one seems to have seen anything." She had been sitting ramrod straight, but now her shoulders slumped a little. "So it looks as if my necklace is really gone, Mrs. Kingsley."

"Odelia, please. And I'm sure my uncle is doing everything he can to return your necklace."

"I should never have kept it at the loft," said Laia, and I could tell she was suffering from the strain of her necklace going missing. "If I'd known..."

"You couldn't possibly know that a burglar would target Jay," said Odelia. She eyed the young woman keenly. "Did you know that Dylon and Jay were in school together?"

"Yeah, Jay told me when the police revealed the burglar's identity." She slumped some more. "There's something I need to tell you, Mrs. Ki—Odelia. Remember I told the police how my parents gave me that necklace?"

"They didn't?"

85

"No, actually I took it." She looked appropriately embarrassed to have to make this confession. "The thing is, when they kicked me out, and said they wanted nothing more to do with me as long as I was intending to marry Jay, I was so upset I decided to take what I felt was mine, which was the necklace. You see, my mother always intended to give me that necklace on the day I got married, only now of course she said she would only give it to me if I married the right person, and obviously since Jay isn't the right person, she was keeping the necklace."

"And so you took it."

Laia bit her lip. "It was a spur of the moment sort of thing. I had gone over there to pack up my belongings—the stuff I still kept at home. And that's when I suddenly remembered the necklace. I knew they kept it in the safe, and I also knew the combination, and when I looked, it was right there. So I just took it, figuring it was mine to begin with. I don't think they even know it's gone."

"Only now that it is stolen, you'll have to come clean."

"Yeah, especially since the insurance will be asking a lot of questions."

"The necklace was insured?"

"Of course. To the hilt."

"The insurance won't like the fact that you took it from a safe place and tucked it away under a pile of your underwear," said Odelia, stating the obvious.

"No, I can see that," said Laia, giving Odelia a miserable look. "Which is why I keep hoping it will turn up. Your uncle told me it might have slipped from the burglar's pocket and ended up in a sewer grate. Though I checked and the nearest drain is twenty feet away from where Mr. Pipe... landed." She grimaced at the memory of the dead man. "So I don't see how it could have ended up in there. But your uncle said workers are going to open the drain and look for the necklace."

"What do you think happened, Laia?"

"Honestly? I think Dylon Pipe wasn't working alone. Jay told me Dylon has a girlfriend, and he thinks they were in this together. Only when Dylon fell she must have escaped before the police got there."

"And taken the necklace with her."

"Yeah, which is what I told your uncle."

"And what did he say?"

"He's going to send some of his officers to talk to her, and search their flat to look for the necklace." She wrung her hands desperately. "Oh, I hope they find it. If they don't, my parents are going to be devastated. And so am I. My parents may be rich, but I'm not. And since they cut me off, that necklace is all I have."

"You were going to sell it?" asked Odelia.

She nodded. "It's worth millions, so I figured I'd sell it and use the money to launch Jay's career as an artist. I believe in him, you see, even if my parents don't. That money could build him a studio where he can work, and hire a manager who will promote his art."

"There's one other thing I need to ask you, Laia," said Odelia, "and you probably won't like it…"

"I think I know what you're going to say. And no, I don't believe Jay had anything to do with my necklace going missing. He and Dylon hadn't seen each other in years. Not since they left school." Twin splashes of color had appeared on her cheekbones and she fervently balled her fists. "Don't you see? I was going to sell that necklace anyway, so there was absolutely no reason for him to steal it."

There was a touch of defiance in her voice, and I could tell that she really loved her fiancé, no matter what her parents or anyone else said. She had their future banking on the necklace, and it being lost was a blow to her hopes and dreams.

"Do you believe he's innocent?" asked Odelia softly.

"Yes," said Laia emphatically. "Yes, I do."

"Then that's good enough for me."

CHAPTER 18

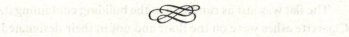

We joined Odelia as she paid a visit to Dylon's girlfriend, per Laia's insinuations possibly the young burglar's assistant in last night's theft.

Laney Basula had apparently just gotten out of bed when we arrived at the grungy little flat she called her own. It was located in a not-very-nice part of town, and looked decidedly dingy. Laney herself was about Laia's age, with flaming red hair and a freckled face. She had bags under her eyes, though, and a sort of sallow tone to her skin that told us she wasn't living life as healthily as she could have.

"She has to take her vitamins, Max," Dooley said when we entered the girl's flat. "She's not eating her fruits and veggies the way she should."

"I'll be sure to tell her, Dooley," I said.

"Well, you should, because if she keeps living like this, she'll get liver deficiency, and then who knows what will happen."

I gave my friend an odd look. "What do you care about Laney Basula's liver?" I asked.

"Well, I saw this documentary yesterday on the Discovery

Channel, and it was all about the liver. The liver is a vital organ, Max. And it's important to keep it healthy."

"I'll make a note of that," I said with a smile in my friend's direction.

"What do you want?" asked Laney, as she rubbed the sleep from her eyes.

The flat was just as rundown as the building containing it. Cigarette ashes were on the floor and not in their designated receptacles, and clothes were on the chairs, not in the hamper where they should be. In a corner of the room a television stood blaring away, showing a wrestling match where grown men were trying to slam each other in painful places. It hurt my insides just to watch them.

"Jay Green sent me," Odelia said.

A flicker of recognition dawned in the young woman's eyes, but then was replaced by a look of suspicion. She lit a cigarette and took a seat at a table that was laden with several Chinese food containers. "So?" she said finally.

"First off, I want to offer my condolences for Dylon's passing," said Odelia.

The girl waved an impatient hand. "Save it, lady. The police were already here, so just tell me what you want and get it over with."

"Dylon stole a very valuable necklace last night, only it wasn't on his person. So now Jay thinks..." She hesitated, and Laney rolled her eyes. Very expressive eyes they were, I have to admit, in spite of the bags.

"He thinks I might have something to do with his precious necklace going missing, is that it? Well, you can tell him from me he's wrong. And next time when he wants to accuse me of something, he should tell it to my face."

"So you weren't working with Dylon last night?" asked Odelia.

"Oh, is that what he thinks? Well, the answer is no. No, I

wasn't working with Dylon. And no, I didn't even know he was going to break into that place. He told me he was doing his modeling."

"What else did he do for a living?" asked Odelia, as she carefully picked a pair of dirty underwear from a chair and lowered herself onto it.

"Dylon was an artist," said the girl with a touch of bitterness, "even though he wasn't really doing a lot with his art lately. He hadn't been able to sell his work, and at some point bills have to be paid, so I told him to get a regular job or else."

"Do you work?" asked Odelia.

"Yes, of course I work. What kind of a question is that? Who are you, anyway?"

"I'm a reporter, actually, but Jay and Laia asked me to sort out some trouble they're having."

"I didn't take their necklace, and I don't know what happened to it. Though if you ask me, I wouldn't be surprised if Jay himself is behind this whole business."

"Jay stole that necklace?"

Laney shrugged. "He and Dylon had been on the phone a lot these last couple of days, and I knew they were up to something, though of course Dylon refused to tell me what it was."

"Jay had been in touch with Dylon?"

"All the time."

"Odd," I told Dooley. "Laia just told us that they hadn't been in touch since they left school."

"So either Jay was lying, or Laia was," said my friend.

"Sounds like Jay was lying to Laia," I said.

"Look, the police have already gone over this place with a fine-tooth comb," said Laney, "which is why the place is such a mess. And they didn't find anything. Or do you think I'd still be here if they had?" She now pointed to Odelia with her cigarette. "You talk to Jay Green. This whole thing smells like an insurance scam to me. And if it is, I hope he rots in jail for what he did to Dylon."

The implication was a tough one, and told us everything we needed to know about what Laney thought really happened last night.

"Time to have a long talk with Jay," I told Dooley.

"She really should take better care of her liver," was my friend's response. "And stop smoking!"

It is true, of course, that this human habit of inhaling smoke into their lungs is a very strange one. Then again, we all know that humans are among the weirdest species on the planet. I mean, who else thinks that watching cats paint is soothing? I certainly don't. On the contrary, I think it's a bad habit, probably up there with smoking and drinking. Can you imagine licking all of that paint from your paws? Paint not being part of the basic food groups it's probably bad for your digestion. And possibly even the liver, but that's Dooley's area of expertise.

Just then, my thoughts were interrupted by Odelia's phone belting out a pleasant tune.

"Laia?" asked Odelia, darting a glance to Laney, who frowned darkly at the mention of Jay's fiancée's name. Odelia listened for a moment, then said, "I'll be there in five."

CHAPTER 19

We arrived at Jay and Laia's apartment in a little more than the promised five minutes, but then I guess when humans say 'I'll be there in five,' they don't actually literally mean five minutes, more a ballpark figure.

Laia had obviously been crying, and Jay didn't look his usual relaxed self either. Clearly something was seriously wrong, apart from the missing of a million-dollar necklace, of course.

"This arrived just now," said Jay, and handed our human a piece of paper.

She read it carefully, frowning all the while, then let it slip from her fingers, so it landed on the floor directly in front of my nose. I quickly scanned its contents, before Odelia picked it up again, with a meaningful look at yours truly.

The letter had a lot of cut out and pasted letters on them, and the message read, 'I know what you did, and I'm going to the police unless you pay me ten thousand dollars. Wait for my instructions.'

"What instructions, Max?" asked Dooley, who'd read the letter as well.

"Probably instructions on how to deliver the money," I said. Which is common practice in cases like these.

We'd been involved in other blackmailing cases, and it usually involved a hollowed-out tree where the money had to be dropped at the crack of dawn. I assumed a similar scenario would be outlined in the blackmailer's next letter.

"I don't get it," said Odelia. "What is this person talking about? What did you do?"

Jay and Laia shared a quick glance, and Laia burst into tears afresh.

"I arranged for Laia's necklace to be stolen," Jay finally admitted, then dropped down onto his couch, unhappily staring before him.

"It wasn't just you, Jay," said Laia. "You have to tell Odelia the truth this time." She turned to Odelia. "We came up with the plan together. We were going to arrange for the necklace to be stolen, then collect the insurance money, and then sell the necklace, or maybe even keep it, since it is an heirloom."

"The insurance money alone would have netted us plenty of money to start our life together with," Jay explained.

"So you asked your friend Dylon to do the honors, only something went wrong," said Odelia.

Jay nodded. "We'd arranged with Dylon that we'd both be out, making sure we had a solid alibi by going to the cinema, where plenty of witnesses could testify that we were there. In the meantime Dylon would break in and steal the necklace. Only somehow he must have slipped and taken a tumble."

"And the necklace?" asked Odelia.

Jay shrugged. "No idea. He was supposed to keep it until the whole thing with the insurance was settled, only the police insists he didn't have the necklace on him, and now it's gone."

"They checked that drain just now," said Laia, "and no

luck. It's not in there either." She gave Odelia a hopeful look. "Did you talk to Laney?"

"I did, and she denies being involved. She did say that she thought Jay was involved somehow, since he and Dylon had been exchanging messages and phone calls so often these past couple of days. Even though you told me Jay hadn't been in touch with Dylon in years."

Laia looked deeply ashamed. "I know. I lied to you, Odelia, and I'm so, so sorry. I just didn't want the police to find out that we were behind the break-in."

"Or the insurance company," Jay added, looking decidedly glum as he fingered the ratty growth on his chin.

"So who do you think this blackmailer could be?" asked Odelia.

"No idea."

"Could it be the same person who is behind this whole stalker business?"

"Maybe," Jay conceded. "Though how could they possibly know about Dylon?"

"Look, you really have to go to the police with this," said Odelia.

"No, but we can't," said Laia.

"Yeah, that's impossible," her fiancé agreed.

"Can't you handle this, Odelia?" asked Laia, almost pleading.

"I'm afraid it's gone too far," said our human. "Now that this blackmailer has joined the fray, the best thing would be to confess everything, and to let the police handle things from now on." And when Laia gave her boyfriend a quizzical look, and the latter was shaking his head, she added, "Just think about it. I'm sure it's for the best if you both come clean now. Before things get even worse."

"How can they possibly get any worse?" asked Jay gloomily. "We've already hit rock bottom." He gave Odelia a weak smile. "Look, I appreciate everything you've done for us, Mrs. Kingsley, but if we go to the police now we'll both end up in prison, so I'm afraid what you're suggesting is simply out of the question."

And that, as they say, was that.

We took our leave, after Odelia had insisted one last time to think very carefully about what she'd said, and to do the right thing this time.

"Why doesn't Odelia want to help this nice young couple, Max?" asked Dooley once we were back in the car and Odelia was talking on the phone with Chase, relaying to him what had just transpired.

"Because she can't engage in any illegal activities," I said. "Since aiding and abetting criminals would make her a criminal herself, and that would open her up to all kinds of trouble. And besides, Odelia is practically a cop, so she can't possibly be instrumental in covering up a crime."

"Still, it's very sad for Laia and Jay," said Dooley, who clearly had taken a liking to the couple, as had I, as a matter of fact. But that didn't make me blind to the fact that they'd committed a crime, and probably should face the consequences.

Chase agreed to hold off on starting an official inquiry for now, giving the couple a chance to come clean, and then we drove back to the office, Odelia to finish up her article, and Dooley and I to take a well-deserved nap.

CHAPTER 20

That night we were all relaxing in the garden, taking in some of those final rays of sunshine before that big benevolent ball of fire in the sky called it a night. Our humans were all gathered around the garden table, discussing the case, and also enjoying a good deal of mild ribbing of Tex and his choice of undergarments, while we cats enjoyed a relaxing time on the lawn, always a nice proposition on account of the cooling properties grass seems to hold, especially after a hot day.

Night soon fell, and the human contingent moved indoors, while we relocated to the paved terrace, which holds warmth a long time after the sun has set, and returns it to those tender underbellies.

And we were just chatting amiably about this and that, as one does, when all of a sudden a masked figure streaked out from Odelia's geraniums, snatched up Harriet, and took off with her!

The whole thing lasted all of two seconds, and before we could respond, Harriet was gone!

"Hey!" Brutus finally cried. "Come back here!"

NIC SAINT

But of course the masked marauder had no intention of returning to the scene of the crime, at least not so fast, and stayed gone. Instead, we all went in search of the man, and our friend, but by the time we arrived at the front lawn, where presumably he'd taken her, a car engine gunned and a sports car of some kind took off at great speed, presumably carrying both cat and snatcher with it!

Brutus made a valiant attempt to race after the car, but soon had to admit defeat against that much horsepower under the hood, and returned to us, panting, and clearly distressed.

"They took her!" he cried, as if we hadn't witnessed the same scene he had. "They just took Harriet!"

"I know," I said, trying to remain calm under the circumstances, and keep a clear head. "Let's tell Odelia so she can call the police."

So we hurried inside, and as soon as we'd relayed our disturbing tale to Odelia and the rest of the company, the powerful machinery that constitutes the long arm of the law cranked into motion like a well-oiled machine. It didn't hurt that Uncle Alec was there, and he only had to bark a few orders into his phone and I imagined a dragnet of epic proportion came crashing down upon our small town, making sure the miscreant wouldn't be able to abscond with our friend.

Or to use Uncle Alec's vernacular: "Trust me, the bastard won't get far!"

"It must be the same guy who came into my office," Odelia said.

"What guy? What are you talking about?" asked Gran.

"Some guy came into my office this morning, wanting to buy Harriet and Brutus. He'd seen her painting video, and offered me five hundred for the cats."

"Hey, a guy offered me two hundred last night."

"Yeah, it's the same guy," said Odelia. "He said you showed him a video of Harriet and Brutus and he thought it was the next best thing since Bob Ross and was going to make Harriet famous." She frowned. "What was his name again?"

"Gallagher Davenport," I supplied.

"That's right! Gallagher Davenport." And immediately she supplied her uncle with this information.

"I'm sending a unit," Uncle Alec growled. "He's not getting away with this!"

"He's a strange one, this Davenport guy," Gran confirmed. "Even though I told him the cats are not for sale, he kept insisting."

"Yeah, same here," Odelia said. She was searching on her phone, typing in the man's name. "Will you look at this," she said, and held up her phone for all of us to see.

On the screen a Persian cat was prancing gracefully against the backdrop of a verdant green garden, a male voice commenting, "The Persian of the species is among the most gracious and intelligent of her ilk. Not only is she the stuff of legend, she is also the most temperamental, and therefore most interesting."

"What's this?" asked Marge.

"It's Davenport's YouTube channel," said Odelia. "He has a channel entirely devoted to Persians."

"Uh-oh," said Gran. "He probably took Harriet so he can add her to his collection."

"But that's wrong!" Dooley cried. "Cats aren't for collecting!"

"I know, Dooley," said Marge, patting my friend on the head. "But it looks like Mr. Davenport didn't get that memo."

"We'll get her back," said Odelia, addressing Brutus, who looked decidedly glum now, staring before him like a cat bereft of his mate, which of course he was.

"I should have stopped him," he said now. "I should have scratched his face."

"He was wearing a mask," I reminded him.

"Yeah, but the least I could have done was scratched his neck or something."

"It all happened so fast. By the time we realized what was happening, he was gone."

"Yeah, he must have prepared his catnapping carefully," said Marge.

Chase and Uncle Alec had left, intent on nabbing the nabber, and Odelia nervously checked her phone for a message from either of the two cops.

"It's possible we won't get more news until tomorrow," she said. "If this guy is smart, he'll lay low for a while."

"I don't get it," said Gran. "What does he hope to accomplish by stealing a cat, for crying out loud?"

"He said he wants to shoot videos of Harriet painting. He told me it's very soothing, and would prove a big hit, because of the combination of painting and cats, both popular topics."

"I think the guy is nuts," said Gran.

Which was also a distinct possibility.

A call came in, and Odelia picked up her phone in seconds. "Chase?" She listened for a moment, then pumped the air with her fist. "Thanks, babe." She hung up, her eyes shining with excitement. "They've just secured a search warrant for Gallagher Davenport's house and they're going in."

"Well, what are we waiting for?" said Gran. "Let's go!"

CHAPTER 21

Gallagher Davenport lived in a biggish house in one of the more posh neighborhoods of our fair little town. It looked like one of those Victorian mansions that England is littered with, an iron fence with sharp spikes protecting the perimeter to keep intruders out —or Persian abductees in. It even had a weathervane on the roof, something you don't see that often. It struck me as a gloomy sort of place, and I fully expected bats to fly out from some attic window, or a creepy ghost to haunt the house and grounds.

"I'll bet he keeps his ancestors in a crypt!" Brutus lamented.

A small police contingent had arrived, and at Uncle Alec's signal, they all marched up to the house, and the Chief did the honors by ringing the bell.

Mr. Davenport soon appeared, dressed in slippers and a velvet dressing gown, a glass of port in his hand and a cigar clenched between his lips. He politely inquired as to the nature of this unexpected intrusion.

Uncle Alec duly showed him the search warrant, and then the cops all swarmed out, in search of our friend.

Dooley, Brutus and I joined the search, and soon were sniffing everywhere, hoping to pick up Harriet's trail.

No such luck, though I did see plenty of Persians... stuffed Persians, that is!

"Yikes!" Dooley cried when we first came face to face with such a specimen. She looked exactly like Harriet, but was obviously long expired. Her mortal remains had been stuffed and positioned on the floor next to what looked like a mouse, who had gone through the same experience and was now stuffed for life.

"This place is hell!" Brutus croaked hoarsely.

"He's going to murder Harriet and stuff her, isn't he, Max?" asked Dooley.

I could only agree that this was a distinct possibility!

Our search carried us into the downstairs area, where the basement had been turned into a large wine cellar, filled with bottles of wine of all description, covered with the requisite spiderwebs, but of Harriet there was no trace.

"I don't smell her, Max," said Brutus as we returned upstairs along the creaky wooden stairs. "I can't smell my sweetheart anywhere!"

"He must have tucked her away somewhere else," I said.

"We have to find her, Max," said Brutus. "We have to find her tonight!"

"Yeah, before he kills her and stuffs her!" Dooley added.

The police were busy searching high and low, judging from the sounds of stomping feet all around us, and since the house was well covered, we decided to take the search operation onto the grounds, something that is often forgotten.

And of course Brutus's prediction proved correct, and before long we found ourselves face to face with a large crypt, on top of which a monument of monumental proportions had been placed, devoted to the Davenport family tree, of which presumably many a member had been entombed beneath our paws.

"Do you think she's down there?" asked Brutus, gesturing to the stone steps that led into the abyss.

"I'm not so sure," I said. I mean, who keeps a cat in a crypt? Only a madman! But we owed it to ourselves to look everywhere, so even though it turned our stomachs, we still headed down into the Davenport family tomb. It was pretty chilly down there, and smelled a little stale, but once more our search proved fruitless, for of Harriet there was no sign.

"It's pretty dead down here," said Dooley, summing up the atmosphere nicely.

Somehow I fully expected a Davenport ghost to raise its voice and warn us off, but nothing stirred, nor man or beast, and we were glad to escape from the place.

Returning to the house, we came upon Odelia, who gave us an inquiring look, but when I shook my head, she shook hers, indicating that so far her search had yielded nothing.

Gallagher Davenport, meanwhile, was still sipping from his glass of port, puffing from his cigar and looking about as placid as a man whose house is being invaded by the constabulary can look.

"I don't kidnap cats, my dear sir," he took great pains to explain to Uncle Alec. "I simply don't. If I want a cat, I pay for it."

"Where were you around nine o'clock?" asked the police chief sternly.

"Why, right here, of course."

"Can anyone vouch for you?"

"My cats," he said.

But when I looked where he was pointing, all I could see was a collection of stuffed Persians!

I shivered. If only he'd had a live cat on the premises, we

could have talked to her, but these were all long past their expiration date!

And then suddenly a lot of phones started ringing: Odelia's phone, Uncle Alec's phone, and Chase's phone. They all took them out simultaneously and glanced at the display.

"Is the search over?" asked Davenport.

"My people will stay here until Harriet is found," said Uncle Alec, much to the man's chagrin.

Odelia turned to us. "Let's go," she mouthed.

"But we haven't found Harriet yet!" said Brutus.

"What's going on?" I asked.

She removed herself from the small group standing in the entrance hall, and lowered her voice. "There's been a murder!" she said.

Oh, dear.

"But I want to stay here," said Brutus. "I need to find Harriet!"

It was a tough call, of course. Chances were that Harriet was still somewhere on the premises, well concealed and out of sight. But if a murder had been committed, and Odelia required our assistance, we couldn't very well turn her down, now could we?

So in the end we told Brutus that we'd deal with this murder business first, and then return later tonight to look for Harriet.

The big cat could live with that, though he said he'd stay there and look on his own. "I'll keep a close eye on this guy, and make sure he doesn't stuff Harriet!"

Now there was something I hadn't thought I'd hear when I woke up that morning.

CHAPTER 22

"**D**o we know who the victim is?" I asked as Chase stepped on it.

Odelia gave her husband a look of significance, then said, "Jay Green."

"Jay Green!" Dooley cried. "But we just saw him this afternoon!"

"Yeah, and now he's been murdered," said Odelia sadly. "And it looks as if Laia might be dead, too. Though that news hasn't been confirmed yet."

"Oh, no," said Dooley. "Laia and Jay!" He shook his head. "They should have listened to you, Odelia. They should have gone to the police when you told them to. And now it's too late."

"We don't know if that has anything to do with this," said Odelia.

"What are they saying?" asked Chase.

"They're shocked about what happened," she relayed our words.

We arrived on Tucker Street, with its now familiar anti-cobblestone posters, and immediately made our way to the loft Jay and Laia shared. Out in front an ambulance idled at the curb, and I saw that Abe Cornwall's car also stood parked nearby. All in all, there was a considerable police presence, and several of the neighbors had stepped out of their houses to see what was going on.

The room where we had spoken to Laia and Jay that afternoon was now a crime scene, the same way it had been the night before, when a break-in had been reported, only now the crime was even more grave.

In the center of the room, right next to the sofa where Jay had been seated when we last saw him, his body now lay in a puddle of blood, though of Laia there was no trace.

"Laia has been taken to the hospital," one of Uncle Alec's officers told us.

"Is she hurt?" asked Odelia anxiously.

"She was found unconscious, but from what I hear she'll live."

"Oh, thank God," said Odelia.

Bent over Jay's body stood Abe Cornwall, his hair looking as lively as ever.

"As if I didn't have enough bodies to deal with," he grumbled.

"So what happened, Abe?" asked Chase.

"It's not pretty," said Abe, casting a warning look in my direction for some reason.

"Best if you guys wait this one out," Odelia announced softly, and ushered us out of the room like a couple of wayward children!

But before we left the room, I picked up a few words that told me she was probably right.

"Battered to a pulp... heavy blunt object... killer must have gone completely berserk..."

"So is he dead, you think, Max?" asked Dooley as we waited patiently in the corridor.

"Yes, I think it's safe to say that he is, Dooley," I said.

"Did his heart give out? Sometimes that happens to young men."

"No, I don't think his heart gave out. He was definitely murdered."

"Oh, my. Well, that's not very nice, is it?"

"Murder rarely is."

I thought my friend took it pretty well, but then I understood his mind was still with Harriet. "We have to get back out there and look for her, Max," he said now. "I mean, it's a sad business, this murder business, but Harriet is still alive, and if we're quick, we can still save her, while Jay is definitely dead, and there's nothing we can do for him anymore, even if we wanted to."

"You're absolutely right, Dooley," I said.

"I am?"

"Of course."

"Brutus will find her, I'm sure of it. He's so determined, he's going to keep looking until…" Then a thought must have occurred to him, for his furry face fell. "Oh, no!"

"Oh, no, what?"

"What if this guy kidnaps Brutus, too!"

"Brutus is not a Persian, Dooley. And Davenport seems to prefer Persians."

"I know, but he is the painter in the family. Harriet is the creative brains, but Brutus is the paws, and the guy said he wanted to buy the both of them, as a set."

He was right, of course. So what if Brutus was in grave danger right now? Then again, would Davenport risk grabbing another cat with dozens of cops trampling all over his house and grounds? He'd have to be nuts to try.

The door opened again, and Odelia joined us, looking very grave, as the situation obviously warranted.

"Well, he was murdered, all right," she said.

"Did they find the murder weapon?" I asked.

"Not yet, but according to Abe it might be one of those cobblestones they're using to repave the road."

"Oh, dear."

"They really did a number on him. Abe said his head is as flat as a pancake."

"Who called it in?"

"A neighbor. He's being interviewed as we speak. But the odd thing is that two calls actually came in. The neighbor's call, but just before that another call."

"How did the neighbor discover the body?"

"The door to Jay's loft must have been open, for his cat had wandered in. He saw the bloody paw prints all over the hallway, and followed them into the loft."

"And what about Laia?"

"No idea. The neighbor found the two of them, Jay obviously badly hurt or dead, and Laia lying right next to him. He actually assumed they were both dead, which is what he told Dolores when he called it in. But fortunately when the paramedics arrived they found a pulse and took Laia straight to the hospital."

Behind her, Chase had appeared, carrying a phone in a plastic baggie. He also carried a grim look on his face. "Look what I found," he said.

"A phone?" Odelia ventured.

"Mr. Green's second phone. There's only one phone number on this one, which has been frequently called. Plenty of messages, too, one even racier than the next."

"Who's the other person?" asked Odelia, understanding immediately dawning on the implication of this find.

He quirked a meaningful eyebrow. "Loretta Everyman."

CHAPTER 23

News had reached our ears—or Odelia's ears at least—that Laia had woken up. So we were in the car on our way to the hospital to talk to her. Chase had decided to stay behind and do some more investigating. He was hoping the loft would yield more interesting finds like Jay's second phone.

"What's sexting, Odelia?" asked Dooley, referring to a term Chase had used to describe the messages Jay had exchanged with his ex-girlfriend.

"Um... well..." She glanced back to me, and I gave her a knowing nod.

"You know what texting is, do you?" I asked.

"Oh, sure."

Well, sexting is like texting, only the messages people exchange are of a more, shall we say, romantic nature."

"You mean like the stuff Harriet and Brutus call each other all the time?"

"Exactly like that," I said, much relieved.

"Oh." He was quiet for a few moments. "So... Jay was

sexting with Loretta, even though she wasn't his girlfriend anymore?"

"No, it now appears as if he was cheating on Laia with his ex."

"That's not very nice. So do you think Laia found out and she killed him?"

It was a conclusion I hadn't yet reached, but sounded like an obvious possibility, so I nodded. "It's certainly possible," I agreed.

"It's one of the things we have to ask Laia," said Odelia, "if she's up to it."

"So was she hurt in the attack?" I asked.

"No, it now looks as if she wasn't attacked at all," said Odelia. "But we'll know more when we talk to her."

We soon arrived at the hospital, and made our way upstairs, to Laia's room, which was being guarded by a plainclothed police officer. Uncle Alec had arranged for the extra security, in light of what had happened to Jay.

We entered the room, and saw that Laia wasn't alone. An older man and woman were sitting by her side, the woman the spitting image of Laia, leading me to assume these were her mom and dad: Algis and Matilda Twine.

"Odelia," said Laia weakly. "I'm so glad to see you. Odelia Kingsley is a friend of me and Jay," she explained to her parents.

At the mention of the despised artist, the Twines directed a pair of distinctly frosty looks at Odelia. Her dad said, "Laia needs to rest, Mrs. Kingsley. Perhaps you can come back some other time."

"You don't understand," said Laia. "Odelia works for the police."

"Oh," said Mr. Twine, as he exchanged a look of concern with his wife. No loving parent likes to see their child being visited by the strong arm of the law.

"Could I have a quick word with your daughter in private?" asked Odelia now.

Reluctantly, the two complied and left the room. And then it was just us and Laia.

"Is he... dead?" asked Laia anxiously.

"I'm afraid so," said Odelia.

"They're not telling me anything," the girl said, and then her face sort of crumpled and she burst into loud sobs.

Odelia supplied her with a paper tissue and a glass of water, and patted her arm consolingly.

"I found him, you know," said Laia finally. "I came home and he was on the floor, and I immediately knew he was dead. Though of course I was still hoping against hope it wasn't true. But there was so much blood..."

"You were also attacked by the same person?"

"No, whoever did this to Jay must have left by then. The door was open, which was strange, and then when I walked in and I found him like that, the world suddenly turned dark. I woke up right here, in the hospital, with Mommy and Daddy by my side, which was just the strangest thing."

"Of course they would be by your side, sweetie," said Odelia. "They're your parents."

"The last time we spoke, we said the most awful things to each other. I didn't think I'd ever see them again."

"I'm so sorry," said Odelia, when the girl started softly weeping again.

"This is all my fault. It must be the same person who sent that blackmail letter. If we'd gone to the police like you told us, this wouldn't have happened."

"You think it was the blackmailer?"

"Don't you? He must have come to get his money, and when Jay refused to pay, he killed him."

"You didn't notice anything suspicious? No one hanging around the loft?"

"No, nothing. And I wanted to go to the police, I really did, but Jay said no. He said that if we went to the police our lives would be over. They'd arrest us for trying to scam the insurance company and we'd both go to prison."

The door to the hospital room opened and Laia's parents walked back in. "I think that's quite enough, Mrs. Kingsley," said Laia's mom, taking the lead. "Our daughter needs to rest."

"Of course," said Odelia. She gave Laia a gentle hug. "We'll talk soon," she promised.

And after casting a final glance at Laia, surrounded by her family, we walked out.

"You didn't tell her about that second phone" I reminded Odelia as we passed along the corridor.

"It didn't feel like a good time to bring that up," she said. "She's had a great shock, and what she needs to do right now is to rest and recover."

And so we drove back to Tucker Street, where the investigation was still in full swing.

Abe had confirmed, based on a preliminary investigation, that the murder weapon was consistent with the kind of heavy granite stone used to repave the street, and when we arrived, Chase was leading a team looking for the murder weapon.

The search ended at the bank of the canal which was located across the street and where he was now staring into the dark pool of water.

"Any luck?" asked Odelia as we joined him.

"I have this hunch that our murder weapon is at the bottom of this canal," he said.

"I talked to Laia, but she doesn't know what happened. When she got here, the killer had already left, and when she saw her fiancé's body, she fainted, which is why the neighbor thought she was dead, too."

"Did you tell her about the second phone?"

"No, she's still in shock from what happened to Jay. It didn't seem like a good time to spring that on her."

"Good call," he grunted as he dragged a hand through his shaggy mane. "Okay, so we better tell your uncle about this whole insurance scam business now."

"Do you think Jay's murder and the scam are connected?"

"It's certainly possible," said Chase.

"Laia thinks the blackmailer is also Jay's killer. That he dropped by the place to make good on his threat and when Jay didn't want to cough up, he killed him."

"Let's put your uncle in possession of all the facts pertaining to the case," Chase suggested, "so he can decide how to proceed." He glanced over to his wife. "Though from where I'm standing Laia has just shot to the top of my suspect list."

"Yeah, I thought she would," said Odelia with a sigh.

"It's not inconceivable that Loretta Everyman was involved in the scam, and that she was the second person who broke in here last night, and grabbed the necklace when Dylon Pipe took a nasty tumble. And if that's the case, it's possible that Jay was trying to scam not only the insurance, but also his fiancée, and was planning to dump her the moment the insurance paid out, and leave town with Loretta. And if Laia found out, she might have flown into a rage and killed him."

"Let's just take it one step at a time," said Odelia, whose heart clearly bled for Laia. "Let's talk to my uncle and see what he thinks."

"And then we have to go back and save Harriet!" Dooley cried, clearly not caring one bit about these humans killing each other over a piece of jewelry.

"Absolutely, Dooley," said Odelia. She looked distracted, though.

Somehow I had a feeling it was going to be up to us to save Harriet from the clutches of her catnapper!

CHAPTER 24

That night, we decided to enlist the assistance of the members of cat choir to organize a search and rescue operation the likes of which Hampton Cove has never seen. Of course when we told our friends what had happened they were all appalled, as they should have been, since this kind of thing can happen to anyone, Persian or no Persian.

"We have to save her from this madman," said Kingman. "If they take Harriet today, they'll come for the rest of us tomorrow, and then where will we be?"

"And as usual you can't rely on the police," said Buster, the hairdresser's cat.

"I think it's a sign of the dangerous times we live in," said Tigger, the plumber's cat.

"It's all those violent video games," was Misty's opinion, the electrician's cat.

"And those violent movies!" said Missy, the landscaper's cat.

"I'm sure it's hormones," said Shadow. She belongs to

Franklin Beaver, the man who runs the hardware store. "There are way too many hormones in human food."

"And I think it's typical that it's a man," said Shanille, cat choir's conductor. "Only men take the trouble to kidnap a female for their own personal enjoyment."

"I think he wants Harriet to feature in videos he'll put up on his YouTube channel," I said. "Painting and such. He says it's very soothing."

"Well, it may be soothing to him, but why should his personal enjoyment require a dear friend to be unlawfully imprisoned like this?" Shanille insisted.

"Oh, no," I said. "You're absolutely right."

"And what I want to know," Shanille continued, "is where Brutus was when all this happened. After all, he's Harriet's partner. He has a duty of care!"

"It all happened so fast that it was simply impossible to—"

"*You* should have been more alert, Max," said Shanille, giving me a censorious look. "I blame it on your diet. It has made you lazy and slow. I mean, who has ever heard of a human that can outrun a cat! It's a disgrace! No, the only reason you were hoodwinked like this is because you were asleep at the wheel."

"Max wasn't at the wheel," Dooley commented, but Shanille ignored him.

"Personally I blame Odelia," she now stated. "And Marge and Vesta. If they had warned Harriet never to talk to strangers, this would never have happened."

"The thing is that the catnapper never actually talked to us," I pointed out.

"It's television," said Missy. "The things they show on television these days. It's all just blood and violence and gore. No wonder humans turn into animals."

"Okay, so maybe we can start our search now?" I

suggested, interrupting these academic discussions, interesting though they were, of course.

"Yes, for all we know, he could be murdering Harriet right now," said Dooley.

That effectively shut everyone up, and so we finally set out for the house of Gallagher Davenport, in search of our dear friend.

We arrived at the spooky place, and the mere sight of that spiked fence did much to discourage the members of cat choir, but of course we're all made of sterner stuff, and so we persisted, and soon were spreading out and covering the grounds, with a large contingent entering the house through the front door, which was still wide open, as the official police search hadn't yet been concluded.

"I wonder where Brutus is," said Dooley as we walked across a creaking wooden floor, sniffing here and there to pick up Harriet's scent, still our best bet to find her.

"He's around here somewhere," I said, sniffing at a particularly old cupboard that must have been built by one of Davenport's forebears.

"Max! Dooley!" suddenly Shanille shouted. "I think I found her!"

We all hurried to join our director, and found her standing in front of one of the stuffed Persians, which managed to look both sad and ominous.

"We're too late," Shanille said in a choked voice. "She's already been stuffed!"

"This isn't Harriet, though," I told her.

"It isn't?"

"No, this guy has plenty of Persians scattered about the place, all stuffed. But none of them are Harriet."

"But if we wait too long, she might get stuffed soon!" Dooley added his two cents to the bargain.

It instilled in us a renewed sense of urgency, and so we spread out once more, poking around here and there.

Finally we found ourselves at the top of the stairs once more, the ones that led down into that wine cellar.

"We already searched down there," Dooley reminded me.

"I know, but we searched every other place in this place, and came up empty-pawed."

"Maybe we missed something?" Dooley suggested, and so we descended those rickety stairs for the second time in one evening, a testament to our persistence.

We found Buster down there, sniffing at a large stuffed Persian, which looked very angry indeed.

"Excellent job," said Buster. "He must have sent her to the pet salon before he stuffed her. Not a single hair out of place. Very nice work." You can take a hairdresser's cat out of the hair salon, but you can't take the hair salon out of a hairdresser's cat, so to speak.

"Max!" Dooley suddenly cried. "Over here! I think I've got something!"

We found him at the back of the basement, near a wall that was covered in some species of green and black moldy residue. It had the consistency of French cheese, though it probably didn't taste like it. But it wasn't the mold that had attracted my friend's attention. It was the wine rack directly in front of it. He was intently sniffing at those wine bottles, like a connoisseur about to open a bottle and take a sniff and a sip, then spit it out again. "Take a sniff," he said, and so I did. And indeed I thought I detected a very familiar scent. The scent of a friend!

"It's this wine rack," said Buster. "I'll bet it covers a door."

"But how to move it?" I asked.

Just then, Brutus came up behind us, looking dusty and tired.

"What you got there, buddies?" he asked.

"We think we found a trace," I told him, and saw him perk up right before our eyes.

"We have to give this wine rack a shove," said Buster. "Can you put your back into it, Brutus?"

"Can I!" the big sturdy cat growled, and immediately put paid to his words by giving the rack of expensive wines such a hefty shove that the whole thing simply collapsed to the floor, dozens of bottles shattering to pieces, and the precious liquid splashing across the old stone floor.

And lo and behold: another staircase loomed before our eyes, a gaping black hole that led down into a deeper level, located underneath the basement.

We didn't hesitate one moment, but immediately descended into the abyss, Brutus leading the way, eager as can be, with Buster picking up the rear.

When our paws hit terra firma once more, we discovered we'd arrived in a sort of dungeon, complete with vaulted ceiling, even darker, dingier and creepier than the rest of the place. What I disliked most was that ceiling: it was blackened with age, and somehow gave me the impression it might collapse on top of us!

But then, as we ventured deeper into the dungeon, I forgot all about the ceiling when I caught sight of Harriet. Our friend was humming... and painting!

CHAPTER 25

$\mathcal{B}$y the light of a single bulb, our dear friend was slaving away at what looked like one of her famous paw paintings. Her otherwise pristinely white paws were now flecked with a multitude of different colors, and against the wall dozens of paintings hung, all painted according to her very unique paw-painting technique.

"Oh, hey, you guys," she said when she finally noticed she was no longer alone. She waved a generous paw, encompassing her surroundings. "Took you long enough to find me! Welcome to my studio. This is where the magic happens! Take a load off your paws, make yourselves comfortable, and watch me create my art!"

And without missing a beat she continued dabbing around and daubing paint across the royally large canvas located underpaw.

"But sugar plum! What are you doing!" Brutus cried, aghast.

"What does it look like I'm doing?" she said, frowning when a certain pawstroke didn't exactly come out as she'd intended. "I'm hard at work on my next masterpiece, that's what I'm doing. Now are you going to stand there or are you going to help me?"

"But snowflake!"

"Don't you snowflake me, Brutus. I thought we had an agreement. I was going to be the creative genius and you my able-bodied assistant bringing my creative vision to life in riotous color. And now look what you've done. You've made me do everything myself!"

"But you were catnapped, sweet cakes!"

"Catnapped? What are you talking about?"

"That man Davenport! He catnapped you and locked you up in his dungeon!"

"He did no such thing. That man is an art lover, one of my greatest admirers."

"But—"

"I'll have you know that when no one believed in me, he was the one who offered me a chance. He built me my very own studio and he has been sponsoring me and pampering me and making sure I can focus on my work. The best food, the nicest smelling litter, the best accommodations. So that I'm not to be disturbed by anything or anyone and I can focus one hundred percent on my art."

"But..."

"Look, if you're just going to stand there criticizing my amazing benefactor, this wonderful patron of the arts, you can just walk right out again."

It was obvious that not only had Harriet been catnapped, but she had also been brainwashed by this man Davenport. I think experts like to refer to this as the Stockholm syndrome, even though Hampton Cove isn't actually located in Sweden, of course. So maybe it was the Hampton Cove syndrome.

"Look, you've been grabbed and locked up here against your own will," I explained slowly, so my words would penetrate.

She gave me a confused frown. "No, I have not. I'm here entirely of my own free will, and look: it's working already. My Facebook page is getting more likes every day, and my YouTube channel is flourishing, and so is my TikTok!"

"But the only person profiting from all of this is Davenport, can't you see!" said Buster.

"And when he's done with you, he's going to stuff you," said Dooley.

"What are you talking about?" said Harriet as she idly stirred the paint in a pot of red paint with her tail, which she had added to the mix to create her unique art.

"Haven't you seen the rest of this place? It's full of stuffed Persians," I said. "There's stuffed Persians on every floor and every room of this house."

"No, to be honest I haven't set paw outside my atelier," said Harriet musingly. "Davenport has this idea that an artist is only able to produce their best work when they're not distracted by the everyday worries that serve to drag us down."

"Look, I think you're suffering from the Stockholm syndrome," I said.

"What are you talking about?"

"What's this Stockholm?" asked Dooley.

"Stockholm is the capital of Sweden," said Buster.

"So? We're not in Sweden," said Harriet.

"You've grown attached to your catnapper," I explained. "To such an extent that you actually think that he's a good person for locking you up and throwing away the key."

"Don't you want to be free again, Harriet?" asked Buster.

"Yeah, haven't you missed me, twinkle toes?" asked Brutus in a raspy voice, dripping with emotion.

His plea didn't fall on deaf ears. "Of course I've missed you. But an artist has to suffer for their art. Or at least that's what Davenport told me. Your true artist can't be attached to anything or anyone that distracts them from the creative impulse."

"He's using you!" Brutus cried. "Using you to make a lot of money!"

"So what's wrong with that?" asked Harriet. "I happen to like lots of money."

"What's wrong with that is that he's not sharing his ill-gotten gains with you, that's what," I said. "Gallagher Davenport is a crook, a gangster, a criminal, a fraud, and he's locked you up down here in this dank dungeon and is making you work like a slave, making a lot of money off your hard work and giving you nothing in return."

Harriet thought about this for a moment. "Well, there is something in what you're all saying, I have to admit. I did wonder why I wasn't allowed to join cat choir anymore. I mean, I am still the number-one soprano, you know."

"Exactly!"

"But Davenport feels that I should drop all my other pursuits so I can focus solely on my painting. No dilution of the creative spark, as he calls it."

"Davenport is going to rot in jail for what he did to you!" said Brutus, making one final passionate plea. "Oh, sweet kitten, come home. I've missed you. We've all missed you. And you can paint as much as you want in the comfort of your own home, with all the creature comforts you're used to!"

"Yeah, there's something in that," Harriet admitted. But she was still not fully convinced, as she gazed at her many works of art she'd created in her atelier.

Suddenly Shanille's voice sounded through the cavernous space. "So this is where they kept you locked up!" the cat choir conductor cried as she joined our merry gang. "Oh, Harriet," she said, and streaked over to our resident *artiste*, and wrapped her paws around her, patting her on the back consolingly. "What *have* they done to you?" She held her at paw's length. "You look absolutely terrible! Paint all over your beautiful fur, your eyes listless and lifeless. I've never seen you look this terrible in all the years I've known you! Poor, poor baby. Poor you!"

Harriet's expression hardened. "This is how an artist is supposed to look, Shanille. And for your information, I'm on a different level now. I'm up there, soaring like the Van Goghs, Monets and Da Vincis of this world!"

"Frankly, you look like crap, Harriet," said Shanille, not impressed. "And if this is what it takes to be an artist, you better drop this foolishness and fast."

Brutus, who'd been leaning against a tall cabinet, now stumbled and inadvertently flicked the lock on the cabinet. It opened and dozens and dozens of stuffed Persians came tumbling out, piling on top of him.

Finally, when he was done screaming, and we'd managed to dig him out from under the pile, I could see that the pile of stuffed cats had had a profound effect on Harriet, as had Shanille's words that she looked like something the cat—a different cat than herself, obviously—had dragged in.

No Persian likes to be accused of looking anything but her absolute best, and Harriet was just such a cat.

What was more, on the inside of the cabinet door, a mirror had been hung, and Harriet took one look at herself, uttered a startled squeal of distress, and said, "You guys—you have to save me! You have to save me from this place—and fast!"

But as she made her way to the staircase, followed by the rest of us, large feet came into view on top of the stairs, and we found our exit barred by a human.

It was Gallagher Davenport, and clearly he wasn't going to let his prize artist leave without a fight!

CHAPTER 26

A sardonic grin spread across the catnapper's face. "More artists for my art factory. Nice!" And in a swift motion, he slammed the door shut behind him so we were all locked up down there with that horrible man, with no avenue of escape!

"I think we're in trouble, Max," said Dooley.

"Yeah, I think you're right," I agreed.

"But I don't want to be an artist!" Buster cried. "I have no artistic skills whatsoever! Unless you consider styling hair art, of course."

"I'm an artist," said Shanille. "Though I very much doubt this man knows the first thing about music. I'll bet he can't even carry a tune!"

"He's going to stuff us," said Brutus. "He's going to stuff us all!"

"I need grooming," said Harriet. "I need a visit to the pet parlor and I need it now! Why didn't anyone tell me I looked this terrible! My nails—my hair—my whiskers!"

These were all sentiments that Davenport, for one, was oblivious to, for as you may or may not know, most humans are impervious to a cat's finer feelings, and most certainly to our excellent skills as engaging conversationalists.

Instead, he forced us to retreat by stomping down those stairs, making us skitter and scatter to all four corners of the dungeon.

"Good," he said. "Just the way I like it."

"I think he's not a Swede but a sadist, Max," said Dooley, who was hiding in one corner with me.

"I never said he was a Swede," I told my friend. "I said Harriet is probably suffering from Stockholm syndrome."

"Well, now we'll all be suffering from Stockholm syndrome," said Dooley. "Unless we find a different exit from this dungeon."

I had a feeling there was no different exit from this dungeon, since dungeons often consist of a big hole dug in the ground, with but a single avenue of egress.

Davenport didn't bother looking for us, or rooting us out from our hiding places. Instead he went stomping back up the stairs. "As soon as the cops are gone, I'm going to put you all to work!" he warned, and then he was gone, slamming the door and bolting it shut for good measure.

"I wish I was a mouse," said Dooley. "Mice always find those nooks and crannies through which to escape. They're very clever creatures, mice."

"Or rats," said Buster, now emerging from his own hiding place, behind an old chair that was missing a leg, seriously hampering its usefulness.

Brutus, who'd hidden behind the pile of stuffed Persians, now also stepped to the fore. "There has to be a way out of here," he said. "There just has to."

"I've looked everywhere," said Harriet, indicating that perhaps she hadn't been as happy in her 'atelier' as she had indicated. "If there is another exit, I haven't found it."

"I'm going to be late," said Shanille. "Father Reilly is going to miss me, and there will be hell to pay."

"Fido is going to be very worried," said Buster. "He doesn't like it when I stay out all night. He likes me to curl up at the foot of the bed, and keep his feet warm."

"He should have taken a dog, not a cat," said Shanille. "Cats aren't made for keeping human feet warm, Buster. That's a dog's job. You disappoint me."

"Oh, but cats can offer that service just as well as dogs can," said Buster. "I'll have you know that—"

"Look, we're not here to talk about the merits or demerits of dogs versus cats," I said. "We're looking for a way out of here, before this man Davenport puts us all to work in his art factory and we never see the light of day again. Ever!"

"We're all going to die down here, aren't we?" Dooley lamented.

"What makes you say that?" asked Harriet. "Davenport has been treating me really well. Plenty of food and drink."

"It's paint," said Dooley. "If you keep licking that paint off your fur the toxins will kill you."

Harriet gulped. "Oh, my God! Tell me it isn't so!"

"It is so," Dooley confirmed. "Paint is toxic, Harriet."

"We already discussed this," I chimed in.

"I need to see the vet!" Harriet cried. "I need to see Vena right now!"

"Isn't a concierge doctor part of the excellent service your Davenport provides?" asked Shanille in a sardonic undertone.

"He's not *my* Davenport, Shanille. He's *a* Davenport. And no, he hasn't yet stipulated that health and dental is part of the remuneration package for his resident *artiste*."

"Let's all spread out and look for an exit, all right?" I said, trying to get us all focused on the same goal once more. "And the one who finds it, gives a holler."

"Gives a holler?" asked Shanille. "Who do you think we are? The Spice Girls?"

"Just... do it, okay?" I said, and set the tone by heading for what looked like a very promising start: that cabinet. As we had seen upstairs, oftentimes cabinets, cupboards and racks are used to disguise an opening. And I hoped this would be just such a cabinet.

"Why the interest in those stuffed cats, Max?" asked Brutus curiously as he followed my progress closely.

"Just looking," I said. I checked underneath the cabinet, behind it, and even inside it, but unfortunately my hunch wasn't playing out the way I'd hoped. Instead, all I got for my trouble was a nose full of stuffed cat hair. Yuck!

"I think we need to enlist the assistance of some denizens of the underworld," said Shanille now, as she, too, returned from an expedition along the dungeon perimeter.

"The underworld?" asked Dooley with a shiver. "That sounds scary!"

"Yeah, what are you talking about, Shanille?" asked Harriet, looking more and more frustrated. The Stockholm syndrome was clearly wearing off, as her more and more frequent passages in front of that mirror indicated.

"We need to talk with someone with an insider's knowledge of this dungeon."

We all stared at her, but she refused to elucidate any further, until she made a beeline for a small scurrying creature that had momentarily emerged from behind a dusty old bookcase, and then disappeared once more. It was small, it was black, and it was not one of nature's most beloved creatures. In other words: it was a black beetle.

"Hey, there, Mr. Beetle," said Shanille, using her most unctuous tone to induce the beetle to emerge once more from its hiding place. "We won't do you any harm," she promised.

"Who would harm a beetle?" asked Brutus with a shudder.

"Some cats love a nice beetle," said Buster. When I gave him a look of astonishment, he shrugged. "Personally I don't move in such circles, and so I don't know anyone who does, but I've heard stories."

"Here, let me try," I said, and approached the small bug with the scurrying feet. "Look, Mr. Beetle," I said, "we're in a spot of bother here. We're..." I quickly counted my co-prisoners, "six cats and we're trapped down here by a very dangerous man who won't hesitate to murder us in cold blood. So if you could please show us a way out, we'd be extremely grateful, dear sir. Or madam."

After a moment, undoubtedly needed for my words to sink in, the beetle came peeking around a corner of the bookcase, drinking me in with its beady little eyes.

"And what's in it for me?" he asked finally, proving that even your common black beetle is a capitalist at heart.

"Well, if you help us," I said, thinking hard, "we'll make sure you have all the food you need for as long as you live." Which, according to some reports, isn't all that long.

"Mh," said the beetle, weighing my offer. "Throw in food for my flock and I'm all yours," he said.

"Your... flock?" I asked. I had no idea black beetles had embraced religion.

"Yeah, I'm the leader of a flock a thousand souls strong, and let me tell you, it's not easy finding nourishment for so many mouths on a daily basis."

"Okay, so I promise you we'll feed your flock of a thousand souls if you can help us escape from this horrible place."

"Would you call this horrible?" asked the beetle, cocking its head a little. "I kinda like it. I mean, it's dark, dank and dirty, which is exactly the way I like it."

Which just goes to show that it takes all kinds.

"So are you going to help us or not?" said Harriet, losing

her patience. "Cause I've got a belly full of paint here, and if I don't see a vet I might die any second!"

"Okay, so if you're prepared to do some digging," said the black beetle, who seemed nice enough once you got to know him, "I can show you a way out."

"That's great," I said. "And we're certainly prepared to do all the digging that is needed. Oh, and by the way, my name is Max."

"Frank," said the beetle. "Nice to meet you, Max." He glanced over to Harriet. "And who's the hot dame?"

"Hot dame!" Harriet cried, a little flustered. "I'll have you know that I've never looked more terrible than I look right now!"

"You still look pretty fine to me, babe," said Frank.

"Why, thank you... I guess," said Harriet dubiously.

Brutus didn't seem particularly pleased with these romantic overtures, but he kept his mouth tightly shut, not wanting to jeopardize our one and only chance of escape.

Frank led us in the direction of an unlit corner of the dungeon, where the ground appeared to have been tilled to some extent.

"This is where we live," he said, and much to my surprise, suddenly that same patch of soil began to move, and before long, dozens of black beetles emerged!

"Flock, meet Max and his friends," said Frank.

"Hi, Max!" said one of the many black beetles who'd joined us.

"Oh, my God, I think I'm going to be sick," I could hear Shanille murmur.

"Okay, so if you dig right here, where the earth has already been prepared," said Frank, "you'll be able to reach the surface in next to no time. It's a tunnel we've built, you see, only of course it's much too tight for you guys. But if you put your backs into it, I'm sure you'll manage." He then heaved a deep sigh. "Of course, in creating your tunnel, you'll also be destroying the place of worship for my flock, which means you'll have to provide us with a new one, same way you're going to provide us with food for the rest of our natural lives."

And when I hesitated to fully and enthusiastically endorse his view on this newly found cooperation between the feline and the coleoptera species, he sternly wagged an antenna at me. "You promised, Max, remember?"

"Oh, all right," I said. "Yes, we'll provide you with room and board on different premises for as long as you all shall live."

"Max, what are you doing!" Brutus whispered in my ear.

"I think I've just promised one thousand beetles that they'll be able to live in our home," I said, and as I said it, I realized this was probably not the best sample of negotiation technique I'd ever displayed. Then again, since our lives were on the line, what choice did I have!

And so on Frank's instructions we all started digging our way to freedom. It took a while, and it took some effort and some planning, but as we all pretended to be moles for a change, and not cats, I'm gratified to say we finally managed to break through into freedom, leaving that dank and disgusting dungeon behind us.

And as we emerged, looking like denizens of the underworld ourselves, our collective fur unfortunately matted and liberally smeared with packed dark earth, a familiar sight met our eyes: it was Odelia and Chase, who at that moment must have decided to drop by once more, to see how the search for Harriet was going.

I almost wept with relief when I saw them walk up to the front door, and cried, "Odelia! Over here!"

Odelia jerked her head around at the sound of my voice, and came hurrying over. And I have to say that when she saw six bedraggled cats staring back at her, their hopeful faces turned up and beaming with joy, she almost wept, too.

"My God, what happened to you!" she cried.

"We escaped from Davenport's dungeon," I explained.

"And Harriet has a Swedish syndrome but she's fine now," said Dooley.

"And Max promised one thousand black beetles that you're going to feed them and give them shelter for the rest of their natural lives," said Brutus.

"You have to take me to the vet, Odelia!" Harriet cried. "He poisoned me! That man poisoned me and now I'm going to die!"

You'll be pleased to know that in the end, Harriet didn't die, and that Davenport was duly arrested for catnapping. Turns out that he'd made stealing Persians part of an MO that went back years, and that many of the cats he'd stuffed had once belonged to citizens of Hampton Cove. In other words, the man was a serial catnapper and stuffer, and had now finally been caught, thanks to the concerted effort of the members of cat choir. A big win for the good guys!

CHAPTER 27

Two big easels had been set up in the backyard of Marge and Tex Poole, and one small one, with the lady of the manor busily putting the first pencil strokes on the canvas that was propped up on her easel. Next to her, her mother was doing the exact same thing, and next to Vesta, Grace was busy with crayons on her own little easel. The birds, who were merrily tweeting on what was shaping up to be a gorgeous morning, had all gathered in a nearby tree to take in the intriguing sight.

Ever since Marge had started her art class, with her mother quickly following in her footsteps, she'd found a renewed purpose in creating her modest works of art. She didn't look upon it as art, of course. Merely as a hobby that had gotten slightly out of hand, but it was definitely something she was good at, or else Chanda Chekhov wouldn't have called her an emerging and promising talent.

"He called me an emerging talent," she now reiterated their teacher's words to her mom, in case the latter hadn't heard.

"You mean like an emerging market?" asked Ma, her

tongue between her teeth as she tried to capture the essence of those birds.

"Laugh all you want. But the fact of the matter is that he believes in my talent."

"Oh, but I believe in your talent, Marge," said Ma. "I believe in it so much that I'm willing to pay good money for one of your paintings, if you ever get it done."

Marge frowned before herself. Her mother had put her finger on a sore point: Marge had started many a drawing, but so far hadn't finished one. It was an area of weakness. She had a vision in her head of how a drawing should look, but then when she studied the end result, she found it lacking in crucial areas. Well, in all areas, actually. Invariably what she drew didn't look anything like the thing she was going for. It was all very frustrating, she found, even though Chanda had told her to be patient, and to work on improving her technique, whatever that meant.

"Look, I've just drawn a bird," said Ma proudly, and when Marge took a peek at her mother's work, she had to admit it actually looked like a bird, unlike her own attempt, which looked more like a potato with a beak.

"If only those birds would sit still for one second," Marge lamented. But of course birds being birds, they just kept fluttering about, darting from tree to tree. No consideration for the poor artist trying to capture them in a drawing.

Meanwhile, Grace was creating her own version of a bird: just a bunch of scribbly lines on her piece of paper. But she was certainly having a lot of fun.

"How are the cats?" asked Ma. "After their terrible ordeal last night?"

"Oh, they're fine. Odelia took them all to the vet this morning, and Vena gave them a clean bill of health. They're pretty shaken, of course, but they'll live."

"Even Harriet? I understood she was force-fed about a gallon of paint."

"That was just Harriet talking. In fact she was smart enough not to lick that paint off her paws, except the odd lick here or there, so she'll be just fine."

"It's horrible how a man like that can operate under the radar for so long."

"Yeah, they should have caught him a lot sooner."

"At least he's not a cat killer," said Ma, frowning as she tried to capture the essence of Marcie Trapper, whose head had just popped up over the hedge to see what her neighbors were up to.

"No, at least there's that," she agreed.

Gallagher Davenport might have kidnapped numerous Persians over the course of his criminal career, but he'd always treated them well, and there was no indication that he'd shortened their lifespan. On the contrary, he loved Persians so much he'd taken great pains to pamper and spoil them. And when finally they reached the end, he'd had them stuffed, which admittedly was a weird thing to do.

"So is Tex going to continue his new career as a model?" asked Ma with a sly grin at her daughter.

Marge could see how Marcie's ears pricked up to take in her reply, so she made sure to enunciate clearly for her neighbor's sake. "No, he's abandoning his career as a model altogether. Once but never again, were his exact words."

"Oh, that's a pity. I thought he was doing a great job. And you have to admit he still looks very good for his age."

"Mh," said Marge, glancing in Marcie's direction, whose head kept moving up and down like a periscope, so as to better eavesdrop on their conversation, and undoubtedly transmit everything that was said to every single person she met.

Just then, a cheerful voice intruded upon the peace and quiet of the art session in progress.

"Yoo-hoo!" the voice caroled, and Marge didn't even have to look up to know they'd been joined by Scarlett Canyon.

"Look what I found in town," said Scarlett, as she produced a rather large portfolio folder, the kind that is used to safely transport drawings and the like. Marge had recently acquired one to house her own work, and so had her mother.

With a flourish, Scarlett produced a sizable painting, and when she positioned it on Marge's easel for her better appreciation, Marge gasped in shock, even as she clutched her neck. "No!" she cried.

"Yes!" Scarlett said.

"Oh, dear," was her mother's response.

It was a portrait of Tex, in all his glory, lying on that stage, looking for all intents and purposes like some latter-day Adonis.

"Where did you get this!" Marge said.

"Oh, they're selling them everywhere now," said Scarlet excitedly. This isn't an original, of course. Just a reproduction, but whoever made this, definitely has talent, wouldn't you say?"

"Yeah, they really captured Tex's..."

"Ma!" Marge snapped.

"I was going to say Tex's essence!"

Just then, Tex came walking into the backyard, munching a bagel. When he caught sight of the portrait, his step faltered, his jaw dropped, and so did his bagel.

"My God," he muttered. "Oh, my God!"

"You're a hit, Tex!" said Scarlett happily. "This is being sold everywhere."

"No," he said in a low voice of horror.

"Yes! They're calling you a sex god. The new Brad Pitt. Tex Pitt, if you will."

Tex made a sort of strangled sound, and suddenly Marge thought she heard a click. When she looked up, she just caught Marcie taking a snap of that painting with her smartphone, then quickly ducking out of sight once more.

Just before Marcie disappeared, Marge caught her big grin. The grin of a neighbor who knows she's about to become the star of her WhatsApp group.

But then a loud scream distracted her. "Now look what she did!" Ma said, and pointed to her drawing. While they were discussing Tex's portrait, Grace had decided to expand her territory, and had been scribbling all over Ma's bird.

"Not bad," said Scarlett. "You are one very talented little girl, Gracie!"

"Brap!" said Grace happily.

CHAPTER 28

While Tex contemplated the consequences of his actions, one backyard over art was the furthest thing from anyone's mind. Harriet, so fervent and excited to become the new reigning queen of the art world, had decided to give up painting altogether, and had taken up to lying on a lounge chair, being waited on paw and paw by Brutus, a treatment she quite enjoyed.

After receiving the good news that she wasn't going to die, she had decided that she'd been given a new lease on life, and so had Brutus, and it was endearing to watch the two of them whisper sweet nothings into each other's ears, and generally behave as love's young dream. Endearing, but also cloying.

Which is why I was happy when Odelia finally was ready to leave for work, and invited me and Dooley to join her, as was her habit.

"Thank God," I said, getting up from my position on the lawn, from where I'd had to endure this lovey-dovey scene for the past hour.

"I think Harriet did swallow too much paint, Max," said Dooley, also getting up.

"And why is that?"

"She's much nicer than usual. That paint must have affected her brain."

"I think she's simply relieved to still be alive," I said. Though it was certainly a nice change of pace that she'd given up painting.

And as we patiently waited for Odelia to call us in so we could hop into her car, we both watched the slow march of a thousand-strong army of black beetles across our lawn in the direction of the fields that are located behind the house.

Odelia, upon learning that we'd made a deal with the beetles, had whimpered a little at the sight of the writhing mass, eager to be taken to their new place of worship. Lucky for us black beetles aren't very picky, and when Odelia had suggested they could take to lodging in the old shed located in that particular field, they had been over the moon. Black beetles apparently enjoy moldy and rotting old wooden structures, and so for them this was paradise.

And we'd just hopped into Chase's car, for today the two of them would join forces and conduct their investigation together, when a call came in on Chase's mobile.

"Yes, Abe?" he said with a frown, for when a coroner calls, it's very rarely with the kind of news that pleases. He listened for a moment, then said, "We'll be there in fifteen minutes," and hung up.

"What's wrong?" asked Odelia, who was buckling herself in.

"I don't know. He wouldn't tell me over the phone. Said he had something important to show me."

"Oh, dear."

It didn't even take us fifteen minutes to get where we needed to be, and when we walked into the coroner's office, which was familiar terrain for Dooley and myself, since we'd been there before, it soon became clear that the coroner's news was very important indeed.

In his small office, Abe had intertwined his fingers on top of a pile of file folders, and fixed Chase with an intent look. "You remember that guy who fell out of a window two nights ago?"

"Sure. Dylon Pipe. What about him?"

"Looks like his death wasn't an accident after all, but murder."

"Murder!" said Odelia.

"Yeah. I didn't notice it when I first examined him, but now that I finally got round to the full autopsy, I discovered that he actually had two head wounds. One is a minor one, consistent with a fall from that window, but the other one is on the other side of his head, and can't possibly have been sustained at the same time, unless he fell once, then bounced and landed on his other side, which is physically impossible." He frowned darkly. "No, it's pretty obvious what must have happened. The kid fell down, hit his head, but wasn't dead. Then someone else came along, and bashed his head in, making sure that this time he was dead."

"Bashed his head in—like Jay Green, you mean," said Chase.

"Yeah, the head wounds are very similar, so I can tell you they were almost certainly made with the same type of object."

"A stone, like the ones found on the street."

Abe nodded, then turned his computer to show us the screen, and proceeded to regale us with a series of pictures of the head wounds of both victims, and pointing out the similarities.

I had to look away, and so did Dooley. Cats are notoriously queasy, or at least we are, and all this blood and gore is the last thing I need in the early morning.

"So two murders," said Chase, finally leaning back.

"That is certainly what the evidence shows," said Abe, well satisfied with his audience's response. Clearly he was a man who thoroughly enjoyed his work.

"Same killer?" asked Chase.

"Now you know I can't answer that, Chase," said Abe with an indulgent smile. "All I can tell you is that the MO is similar."

"So what does that mean, Max?" asked Dooley.

"That means that first Dylon was killed, and the next night, his friend and co-conspirator Jay. Possibly by the same person, and the same murder weapon."

"Coincidence?" asked Chase. "I think not."

And that was my conclusion also. Two friends conspiring to scam the insurance, both ending up dead, killed on consecutive nights. And the necklace the whole thing revolved around? Still missing. So could the murderer of both men also be the person who stole that necklace and still had it in their possession? It was an interesting question, to be sure. And one we had to find an answer to.

CHAPTER 29

In the car, Odelia and Chase discussed the case, and how they needed to proceed, taking this new evidence into account.

"This whole case seems to hinge on that necklace being stolen," was Odelia's opinion. "So whoever took that necklace is probably also the killer."

"Must be the person Dylon was using as an accomplice."

"Or it could be someone completely unconnected to the case," said Odelia. "Suppose someone was walking their dog that night, and saw Dylon take a tumble from that window. And suppose the necklace slipped from his pocket when he fell, and was just lying there, on the street. So what if this person decided, in a spur of the moment sort of thing, to pocket the necklace?"

"Yeah, but why kill Dylon?"

"Maybe Dylon wasn't unconscious? And when this person picked up the necklace he tried to stop them, and so the thief killed Dylon in the struggle?"

"And then returned the following night to kill Jay?"

"He could be the same person who was trying to blackmail Jay, and maybe Jay met up with the guy, behind Laia's back, and they had an argument?"

"A lot of maybes, babe," said Chase. "I still think it's a lot more plausible that Laia is the killer. Somehow she found out that Jay was cheating on her with his ex-girlfriend and so she decided to put a stop to that once and for all."

"She doesn't strike me as a killer," said Odelia thoughtfully. "Though I can see how that would make sense, of course."

"Though if it was Laia, she couldn't have possibly killed Dylon," said Chase, walking back on his own theory. "I checked with the cinema and she and Jay were definitely at the movies two nights ago."

"Okay, so let's look at this methodically," Odelia suggested. "And take motive into account. Bud Zuk was upset with Laia for dumping him, so he could have decided to get even by stealing her necklace."

"Sounds like an iffy motive for a double murder, babe."

"Unless we're looking at two different murderers."

Chase groaned and rubbed his face. "Okay, keep going."

"The problem is that Bud sprained his wrist, though he could be faking it, of course."

"Or he could have killed Dylon with his left hand instead of his right."

"True. And then there's Laia's parents, who hated her new boyfriend with a vengeance, and wouldn't have minded seeing him dead."

"Yeah, but would they steal back their own necklace? And why kill Dylon? They probably don't even know the kid."

"Okay, but we still have to go talk to them."

"Yeah, we have to talk to all of them," said Chase, as he started up his engine.

The Twine residence was an impressive manor, and we were invited to join the lady and master of the house in the living room, where we were also greeted by Laia Twine, who still looked a little pale and wan, but otherwise in fine fettle.

"I'm glad to see you're all right, Laia," said Odelia warmly.

"Yeah, I got discharged this morning," said Laia. "The doctors said I suffered a great shock, but apart from that there's nothing physically wrong with me."

"All she needs is a lot of rest and a lot of TLC," said Matilda Twine, who took a seat next to her daughter on the couch, and patted her hand warmly. "And we've got that covered, don't we, sweetie?"

Algis Twine looked the most alive of the bunch. His face was flushed, and he had an apron tied in front of his rotund belly. Traces of flour were covering his shirt, and even his upper lip, and he announced cheerfully, "I'm making pancakes, in honor of our little girl who's decided to move back home! Want some?"

Chase and Odelia both made confirmative noises, and the man disappeared again, to whip up some more pancakes.

"So you've decided to move back home?" asked Odelia.

"After what happened, I couldn't stay in that place one minute longer," said Laia, and shivered convulsively at the thought. "Anyway, it was Jay's place, not mine."

"So could you tell us what happened exactly, in your own words?" asked Chase.

"Is this really necessary?" asked Matilda.

"It's fine, Mommy," said Laia. "I want to help them catch whoever did this to Jay." She frowned as she threw her mind back. "Like I told you last night, I walked into the room and found him lying there, in a pool of blood, and I knew immediately that he was dead. I must have fainted, for when I woke up—"

"At the hospital," Chase supplied.

"Well, yes, but since I saw you last night, I've been thinking, and now I remember that I must have woken up briefly while I was lying there."

"Honey, you didn't tell us about that," said her mom.

"No, because I thought it was just a dream, but now I'm thinking it must have been real." She shook her head, as if trying to clear away the cobwebs. "I was lying there, and I distinctly remember someone leaning over me, and putting a finger to my neck, and now I'm thinking that whoever it was was trying to check my pulse."

"Did you see this person's face?" asked Odelia.

"No. I think they were wearing a mask. I'm not sure. I was half unconscious, which is why I first thought it must have been a dream, but the more I think about it, the more convinced I am that it must have been real."

"If this person was leaning over you soon after you discovered Jay's body," said Chase gravely, "then that person could have been the murderer, Laia. Especially if they were wearing a mask."

The girl shivered again, and nodded. "I know. Which is why I wanted to be sure before I told you."

"Oh, sweetheart," said her mother, and stroked a strand of hair from her daughter's face. "You're safe now." She turned to Odelia. "One other reason why it's better for her to stay here. What if the person who killed Jay decides to return?"

"Yeah, I'm never going there again," said Laia decidedly.

"There's something else we need to tell you, Laia," said Odelia. "And this might come as a shock."

"Oh, please, no," said Matilda sternly.

"Mommy, it's fine," Laia repeated. "Yes, what is it?" she asked, with a touch of trepidation.

"Jay had a second phone," Chase explained. "Did you know about that?"

"A second phone? No, I didn't know that."

"He used it to exchange messages and calls with Loretta Everyman."

"I knew it!" Matilda cried, slapping her thigh.

"Mommy!"

"I told you that man couldn't be trusted, didn't I?"

"So Jay was still in touch with Loretta? Is that what you're saying?" asked Laia.

Odelia nodded. "Looks like they were still very much... together."

"The texts they exchanged are pretty, well, steamy," Chase said.

"The scoundrel!" Matilda cried, getting up and pacing the room.

Laia looked taken aback by this news. "So Jay was cheating on me with his ex?"

Both Odelia and Chase nodded.

"God," said Laia, looking away. "I'm such a fool."

"When we look at the messages it's obvious that Jay was planning to take possession of the insurance money you were hoping to get for the necklace, and then leave town together with Loretta."

Odelia looked at Matilda, but the latter simply nodded and waved an impatient hand. "I know about the necklace," she said. "Laia has decided to come clean and tell us about the whole sordid business. We know it was all Jay's idea."

"So Jay was going to take that money and leave me?" asked Laia, looking crestfallen.

"Yeah, I'm afraid so," said Odelia. "I'm very sorry, Laia."

"God, he really played me for a sucker, didn't he?"

"Yes, he did!" her mother said emphatically. She then addressed Chase, just as sternly. "I hope you'll have a good long talk with this Loretta. Seems to me she's the person you should be looking for in connection to Jay's murder and the theft of the necklace both!"

"Why would Loretta kill her boyfriend?" asked Chase. "They were planning to go away together once the insurance paid out."

"They must have had a fight. Happens all the time. He decided to break up with her and hitch his wagon on Laia's ride and so Loretta killed him in a fit of rage."

"We're definitely going to talk to Loretta," said Chase, "but there are other suspects."

"What suspects?" Matilda demanded.

"Well, we've now discovered that Dylon Pipe's death wasn't an accident. He was murdered."

"Dylon was murdered?" asked Laia, shocked by this piece of news.

"I'm afraid so," said Chase. "So now we're looking at two murders, on two consecutive nights, presumably both in connection to your stolen necklace."

"Which you people still haven't found," Matilda reminded them.

"Which brings us to another aspect of the case," Chase went on without acknowledging Matilda's outburst. "Dylon Pipe had a reputation in this town for being a low-level drug dealer."

He arched an inquisitive eyebrow in Laia's direction, who sputtered, "Well, obviously I didn't know that, Detective."

"Why are you looking at my daughter like that?" Matilda demanded. "She had no involvement with this Dylon Pipe character whatsoever. He was Jay's friend, not hers."

"You didn't know Dylon was dealing, Laia?" asked Odelia gently.

Laia shook her head. "Absolutely not. If I had, I would have told Jay to cut all ties with him."

"Of course my daughter didn't know," said Matilda. "We raised her better than to associate with drug dealers and other riffraff."

"What riffraff?" asked Algis, who now entered carrying a plate with steaming hot pancakes. He had even more flour smeared all over his face and front.

"Jay's best friend was a drug dealer," said Matilda. "The one who stole my necklace."

"My necklace," Laia corrected her mom.

"Right now it's still my necklace," Matilda insisted. "At least if I ever get it back. Probably one of that drug addict's friends must have taken it, and bashed Jay over the head in the process."

"You're so lucky you got out of this business with your life, honey," said Algis.

"I know, Daddy. And I'm sorry about the necklace."

"Oh, that's all right," said Algis.

"Oh, so *you* think it's fine, do you?" asked Matilda.

"It's just money, honey! The main thing is that we've got our little girl back."

Matilda didn't seem to be fully in agreement, but she didn't say anything. Laia continued to look stricken and apologetic, and I didn't wonder. Not only had she lost her mom's expensive necklace, she had also dragged her family into what now looked like a gang of crooked friends and associated drug dealers, and had risked her own life in the process.

"I'll tell you what happened," said Matilda, crossing her arms in front of her chest. "Jay and Dylon were killed by gangsters. I mean, everyone knows that these drug people are always killing each other, so that's what must have happened." She eyed her daughter fixedly. "Promise me never to go back, sweetheart."

"I already told you, Mommy. I didn't know Dylon was a drug dealer."

"And it wouldn't surprise me if Jay was a drug dealer, too."

"Okay," said Chase, eager to wrap this up. "One last thing we need to ask: can you tell us where you both were last night?"

It took a moment for Algis and Matilda to realize he was addressing them, but when she finally did, Matilda burst out, "You're not accusing *us* of murdering that good-for-nothing drug addict, are you!"

"I'm not accusing you of anything, Mrs. Twine, but these are routine questions that need to be cleared up."

"Well, I never," said the woman, giving Chase a look that could kill.

"It's all right," said Algis. "We were both here last night, watching television, until that dreadful call came in, telling us that our little girl had been taken to the hospital."

"The biggest fright of my life," said Matilda, clutching at her neck.

"And where were you last night, Laia?" asked Odelia.

"Why do you want to know where my daughter was?" asked Algis, who'd been sampling one of his own pancakes, eagerly gobbling it down in one piece.

"Yes, hasn't she suffered enough?" demanded Matilda, planting her hands on her sides.

"I was out with a friend last night," said Laia quietly.

"Name of that friend?" asked Chase dutifully. And when Laia had supplied the information, plus the friend's phone number, in spite of her mom and dad's protestations, Chase closed his notebook and nodded to the girl. "Thank you for your cooperation, Miss Twine."

"Will that be all?" asked Matilda with a touch of belligerence.

"Here, have a pancake," said Algis, holding up the plate. "They're fresh!"

But his wife snatched the plate away. "There will be no pancakes," she said. "Not until you've apologized for accusing us of these monstrous acts of villainy."

"Mommy! They're simply doing their job!" Laia said.

"Well, they should be doing a better job," Matilda insisted stubbornly. "And bring me back my necklace, for a start!"

I think it's safe to say we were all glad to finally leave the company of the Twines and drive away from the place.

"Now I understand why Laia decided to leave home," said Odelia as she blew out a sigh of relief.

"Yeah, Matilda Twine is a pretty tough baby," Chase agreed.

"Why didn't we get to have a pancake, Max?" asked Dooley.

"For one thing, pancakes are full of sugar, and therefore not very good for cats, Dooley," I said. "And for another, Laia's mom didn't want us to have any pancakes."

"But why not?"

"Because she doesn't like us very much. She thought we were accusing her daughter of murder, and that's not something a mother enjoys."

He thought about this, then said, "I think she was right. It's not a lot of fun when people drop by and accuse you of murder."

"We didn't actually accuse her of anything," I said. "We just asked her some questions, trying to shed some light on past events."

"Yes, but still. If someone dropped by the house and accused Grace of being a murderer, Odelia wouldn't like it either, and Chase wouldn't bake them any pancakes."

I smiled. "I don't think Grace is capable of murder, Dooley. She's too young for that sort of thing."

"She did murder Gran's drawing this morning."

"That, she most certainly did." Though some would say she actually improved on Gran's work. But I'd never say that out loud, of course.

I didn't want to become the victim of caticide, you see.

CHAPTER 30

Once more we found ourselves at our local supermarket, though this time, with the presence of Chase, the interview had a slightly more formal aspect. No more standing in line at the checkout counter, and hoping Loretta Everyman would be gracious enough to give us the light of day. This time we caught the young lady on her smoking break, standing outside at the back of the supermarket, right next to the gate where a ten-ton truck was being unloaded.

"Now what do you want?" asked Loretta, as friendly and forthcoming as before.

"Chase Kingsley," said Chase, flashing his badge. "Hampton Cove police. And I believe you've already met my wife Odelia. We wanted to ask you a couple of questions, Miss Everyman."

Loretta still looked as if she'd just sucked on a lemon, but at least she became more talkative. The miracle of the badge, I guess.

"Okay, so, yeah, Jay and I were still an item," she admitted when confronted with her boyfriend's text messages—or sext messages, as the vernacular goes. "But that doesn't mean I killed him. I mean, why would I do such a crazy thing? I loved the guy, for crying out loud. I would never hurt him."

"Is it true that you were planning to leave town once the insurance paid out the money for the necklace?"

"Yeah, that was the plan," she said, then sighed. "Or at least Jay's plan. I never said I agreed with it. It seemed a little rough on Laia, and probably criminal. The Twines are a pretty powerful family around here, and I'm sure they would have come after us if we'd taken that money." She frowned into the middle distance. "Which is why I've taken my precautions."

"What do you mean, precautions?" asked Odelia curiously.

"Well, they got to Jay, didn't they? And they're bound to come for me next."

"Who's coming for you?"

"The Twines, of course. Who else? They know we stole from them, and now they're getting even."

"But... you didn't take the necklace, did you?" asked Chase, confused.

"No, of course not. That was Dylon's job. He was supposed to steal the necklace, Jay was going to deal with the insurance, and then we were going to skip town with the money, and make sure the necklace ended up in Laia's hands again. So the Twines wouldn't come after us. But then the whole thing fell apart. First Dylon died, then the necklace went missing, and then they killed Jay."

"The thing is, Loretta," said Odelia, "that we now have reason to believe that Dylon was also killed, and possibly by the same person who killed Jay."

Loretta stared at her for a moment, her mouth open, then

she snapped it closed, a determined look in her eyes. "Well, that does it. If you don't give me police protection now you'll have the blood of an innocent woman on your hands pretty darn soon."

"What do you mean?" asked Chase.

"God, man, do you have to spell it out for you? They killed them both! First they murdered Dylon, for stealing their necklace, and then Jay. And that necklace is safely back in the family vault by now." She snapped the ash off her cigarette. "Don't mess with the Twines. The message is clear now, isn't it?"

"But how would the Twines know about the plan you and Jay and Dylon were hatching?" asked Odelia.

"I don't know. But they must have found out somehow. Maybe Dylon blabbed, and word got back to the Twines, or maybe Laia told her mommy and daddy, and they decided to intervene." She narrowed her eyes. "Though now that I think about it, it could have been Laia herself. If she knew about me and Jay. I mean, you know what those rich girls are like. They think they can get away with murder."

"Laia has a solid alibi for both murders," Chase pointed out.

"Then it was the Twines. Mark my words, if they're not stopped, more killings will happen, with me number one on their hit list."

It all seemed a little far-fetched, and I had the impression she was trying to cover her own part in the scheme. Which is perhaps why she got so belligerent when Chase asked where she was last night and the night before.

"What are you harassing me for! I didn't do this. Go talk to the Twines!"

Which probably was her way of telling us she didn't have an alibi.

Her smoking break was at an end, and her manager came looking for her, insisting she went back to work.

"Well? Aren't you going to arrest me?" she asked, holding out her hands and offering her wrists.

When Chase declined to offer her the courtesy of a fine set of manacles, she made a scoffing sound and returned inside.

"Nice attitude," said Chase once Loretta was gone.

"Yeah, she's not exactly cooperative, is she?"

"Let's just put this one in the no alibi column."

"She made the Twines sound like a family from *The Godfather*," said Odelia. "Which doesn't strike me as being the case."

"No, Algis Twine isn't exactly Don Corleone," Chase said with a smile. "Unless he's taken to baking pancakes for his gang." He checked his watch. "Talking about gangs, I think it's time we had a little chat with Tyrone Friday."

"Who's Tyrone Friday?" asked Odelia as we headed back to the car.

"I'm glad you ask," said Chase as he placed an arm around his wife. "Tyrone is, or was, Dylan's supplier. Though we've had a hard time pinning anything on him. Tyrone is by way of being a local kingpin in the drug trade. And so if anyone knows what Dylan was involved in, it would be Mr. Friday."

"A real gangster," said Odelia. She glanced down at us. "Maybe I should leave the cats in the car for this one."

"Not a chance!" I cried.

"I want to see the drug kingpin!" Dooley yelled.

"Oh, don't worry," said Chase. "Tyrone wouldn't hurt a fly. It's the people who work for him you should worry about, not Tyrone himself, who's a real pussycat."

"Tyrone is a pussycat?" asked Dooley, confused. "Gee, I had no idea that a cat could also be a drug kingpin, Max." Then he added, "What is a drug kingpin?"

"The man in charge of the local drug trade," I said. "In other words, the big honcho, the big cheese, the man up top."

"Can't wait to see him," said Dooley. "Maybe we can invite him for cat choir."

CHAPTER 31

Turned out that Tyrone Friday owned a restaurant that was called, very uninspired, I thought, Tyrone's Place. And it was there that we found the big man.

Chase explained that most criminals of Mr. Friday's level own many legal businesses, which they use as a front for their criminal activities, and also to launder some of that black money they make by selling drugs and other stuff.

Tyrone himself was a very nice guy of about Tex's age, looking more like a favorite uncle than a drug kingpin.

"Oh, Mr. Kingsley!" he said the moment we set paw inside his place of business. "Come in, come in! What can I offer you?"

"I'm good, thanks," said Chase, holding up a hand in defiance of the man's hospitality. "I'm afraid we're here on official police business, Tyrone."

"Well, isn't that too bad. I really was hoping this was a social call."

The man had one of those round faces that was surrounded by a fringe of hair all around, and a sort of stripe in the middle that was his mustache. It made for a nicely symmetrical view, which is always pleasing to the eye.

"So what's this about?" asked Tyrone, once we are all seated at his table. Well, the humans were seated, while Dooley and I remained with our paws firmly on the floor.

"Dylon Pipe," said Chase curtly.

"Oh, terrible business," said Tyrone, shaking his head. "Such a waste. He was a great talent. In fact I own several of his paintings." He pointed to a painting that hung just above us. It was a beach scene, with many colorful umbrellas. It wasn't much to look at, but then of course I'm not an expert. "An original Dylon Pipe," said Tyrone proudly. "And of course, sad as it makes me to say this, it will probably increase in value now that the artist has died." He spread his arms, palms upward. "But then I guess such is life."

"You don't think he killed Dylon just so he could make his paintings go up in value, do you, Max?" asked Dooley.

"I doubt it, Dooley. For one thing, I don't think Dylon's work is all that valuable to begin with. And a hundred percent increase of nothing is still nothing."

"Rumor has it that Dylon was doing more for you than merely decorating your restaurant, Tyrone," said Chase.

"Oh, that's right. He worked the kitchen from time to time. Dishwasher, you know. The kid couldn't cook, but he could wash a mean dish." And he grinned widely, as if he'd just told the funniest joke.

"You know what I mean."

Tyrone quickly sobered. "Look, Detective, suppose just for a moment that Dylon did work for me in the capacity I think you're implying, now why would that be relevant to the way he died?"

"Because your line of business isn't exactly without risk, is it, Tyrone?"

"The restaurant business?" he asked innocently. "No, I

guess you could say there's some risk attached to what I do. Plenty of competition and a fickle clientele."

"Oh, cut the crap, Tyrone. You know perfectly well what I mean."

The restaurateur smiled a fine smile. "Okay, so suppose I do know what you mean, now why would I be implicated in that young man's death?"

"You tell me."

"No, you tell me. Give me one good reason why I would want Dylon dead."

"Maybe he owed you money?"

"And why would I murder a man who owed me money? Dead men don't pay, Detective. So that would be a very stupid thing to do, wouldn't you agree?"

"Okay, so maybe he stole from you? Took more than he was owed?"

"Once again, what would I gain by killing a man, even if he did steal from me? Wouldn't it be a lot smarter to make him pay up?"

"You could be sending a message to some of your other... collaborators. To discourage them from doing the same thing?"

"Look, I know what you're driving at, Detective," said Tyrone, rubbing his rather rotund belly, "but I can assure you, this is no way to do business. At least it's not the way I do business. If someone steals from me, I don't go around bashing their brains in. It doesn't work like that. Do I make sure they compensate me? Of course. But I do so in a civilized manner. Not with murder!" And he laughed, as if the mere notion was ludicrous, which perhaps it was to him.

He certainly didn't look like a vicious killer. More like a fun Santa Claus.

"Look, I can see that you're stuck, Detective," said Tyrone finally. "Which is why you came to me. Because if you weren't stuck, you'd know that I couldn't possibly be involved in this nasty business. And now I hear a second man was murdered." He shook his head. "Absolutely not my style. So I'm going to do you a favor. I'm going to give you the name of the person I think might be involved." And he took a piece of paper and wrote down a name and slid it across the table.

"Bronson Shagreen?" asked Chase. "Who's he?"

"An artist, like Dylon. And from what Dylon told me, not his biggest fan."

CHAPTER 32

We found Bronson Shagreen, the artist, at Town Hall, where he was instrumental in creating a unique work of art to enliven the main atrium, the place most citizens see when they pay a visit there for Town Hall business.

When we arrived, Charlene was there to welcome us, and introduce us to Bronson. The young man was standing on a scaffolding, which covered the entire atrium wall, and was painting something near the ceiling. It was hard to see what it was, but once it was finished, Charlene said it was going to blow us all away.

"I probably shouldn't say this," said Charlene, "but originally Jay Green won the competition, but when he died we decided to give Bronson a chance. And his work is just amazing. I actually thought he was far superior and more suitable than Jay, but I wasn't the only member of the jury, and the majority always decides. So in a sense Jay's death was a blessing in disguise."

"What competition?" asked Chase.

"The town council organized an art competition," Odelia

explained, who had written about it. "To find the most promising local young artist. The winner gets to create an art installation right here at Town Hall, and his work will be publicized in the council newsletter."

"Great publicity for the artist," said Charlene. "And for Hampton Cove, of course, since it will put us on the map as the artistic capital of Long Island."

"And so Jay originally won the competition?" said Chase, exchanging a look with his wife.

"Yeah, some people thought he was great, but I wasn't one of them. I always thought his work was too pat. Too slick. Of course it's all a matter of taste, isn't it?"

Bronson, who had climbed down from his high perch, greeted the newcomers with a pleasant grin. He was clean-cut and athletic, and didn't look like any artist I'd ever seen. More like a sportsman. Though of course one didn't exclude the other.

"Chase and Odelia are with the police department," Charlene explained, making the necessary introductions. "And they would like to ask you a couple of questions about the death of Dylon Pipe and Jay Green."

Just then, Gran walked in, carrying a large portfolio folder under her arm. When she saw Charlene, she made a beeline for the Mayor. "Glad that I caught you," she said. "I want to apply for that new grant."

"Oh, that's... great," said Charlene, reluctantly accepting the large folder from her boyfriend's mom. "What is it?"

"A nude," said Gran. "I think you'll like it," she added with a wink.

Charlene swallowed a little convulsively when she saw that it was actually a nude portrait of Odelia's dad. "Did you paint this?" she asked.

"Of course I painted this. What do you think?"

Charlene touched her hand to the painting. "It doesn't feel like an original."

"Well, it is. I had another one ready to go, a real masterpiece, but *her* daughter ruined it." At this, she directed a disapproving glance at her granddaughter.

Charlene grimaced, and quickly tucked the painting away again. "Well, thanks, Vesta. I'll certainly take your candidacy into consideration."

"What are you talking about? You can see this is an excellent piece of original art, so you can give me my grant right now. I could use the money."

"It doesn't work like that and you know it, Vesta," said Charlene. "But I'll certainly add you to the list of candidates. The *long* list of candidates," she added.

Gran grumbled something that wasn't fit for print, then stalked off.

"What grant is this?" asked Chase.

"Oh, it's a new project we're launching in conjunction with Bronson's art installation. We're integrating the work of local artists all across town, in many different locations, and so we're looking for candidates to put their work forward. Auditions run for three months, and a dozen artists will be chosen who can pick a spot, in consultation with a panel of experts, of course, to display their work."

"I think it's so great you're doing this," said Bronson. "A very novel approach."

"It's important that we keep trying to make Hampton Cove stand out as the jewel in the Hamptons crown that it is," said Charlene with a touch of pride. "Okay, so I'll leave you to it, then," she added, and started to walk away. But just when she did, Scarlett walked in, also with a large portfolio folder under her arm, which she handed to the Mayor. Charlene opened the wallet, caught a glimpse of yet another partially nude Tex Poole, blanched, and closed it again. She plastered a polite smile onto her face. "Thanks, Scarlett. I'll be sure to add you to the list."

"That's all I ask," said Scarlett. "Though I think you'll find that I've created a unique work of art that really captures the spirit of Hampton Cove perfectly."

"Yes. Yes, I can see that," said Charlene, though she seemed a lot less sanguine about the uniqueness of this spirit than the artist in front of her.

"Well, see you," said Scarlett, and gave us all a cheerful wave and was off again.

Finally Charlene walked away with some difficulty, since she now had to carry two large portfolio folders, both containing what I was almost certain were the same reproductions that were for sale all over town right now. One person had apparently snapped a picture of Tex two nights ago, had turned it into a painting, and was selling prints of the doctor's portrait to anyone who wanted it.

"Bronson," said Chase, as he directed his attention to the young artist.

"Detective?" said Bronson anxiously. No one enjoys a police interview, and Bronson Shagreen was obviously no exception.

"What are you painting?" asked Odelia, trying to break the ice a little.

"Now that would be telling, wouldn't it?" said the artist with a smile.

"I wonder if he'll do the ceiling, too," said Dooley. "Like Michelangelo? He did a fine job at that Sistine Chapel, didn't he?"

"What do you know about Michelangelo and the Sistine Chapel?" I asked.

"Well, there was this documentary about him. Gran saw it, too, and she said if a useless dauber like Michelangelo could attract so much attention by splashing some paint across some ceiling, she'd have no trouble blowing him out of the water with her own work. Which I guess she just did, with her contribution to this grant business."

"I think her contribution won't blow anyone out of the water," I said dubiously.

"So we have it on good authority that you and Dylon were great friends?" said Chase, opening proceedings.

"I wouldn't say that," said Bronson. "More acquaintances. We met in art school, you see. Me and Dylon and Jay were all in the same class, and we also applied for this same installation," he said, gesturing to the ceiling-high scaffolding.

"So you and Dylon and Jay were in competition over this art installation?"

"Yeah, but it was a healthy competition, I can assure you."

"Which Jay Green won."

"Which Jay won, with Dylon second and me third."

"Plenty of prestige associated with such an installation, I imagine?"

"Oh, absolutely. When you can show your work to such a large audience, it's always interesting for a new artist. And of course we're hoping the media will turn up en masse for the big opening." He directed a hopeful smile at Odelia, our resident reporter. But then the meaning of Chase's words registered. "Oh, you're suggesting I killed Jay and Dylon so I could take first place in the competition?"

Chase didn't respond but merely crooked a meaningful eyebrow.

"But that's simply absurd," said Bronson. "I wanted to win, sure, but I would never murder my friends."

"But you just told us they weren't actually your friends."

He wiped away a bead of perspiration from his brow. "Look, I'll be honest with you, Detective. Me and Jay didn't get along very well. I admit that."

"And why was that?"

"Jay was... I want to say, a grifter? Always looking for an angle, you know. Always looking for a way to get rich. All he talked about was becoming rich and famous one day. While for me art isn't a way to get rich quick. It's more a way of life. Of course I would love it if I could create the kind of art that is appreciated by a large audience, but if it isn't, that's all right, too. But to Jay the only reason he became an artist was to be fabulously wealthy, and that didn't sit well with me."

"And Dylon?"

"Dylon was all right. I liked him. Though he did have substance abuse issues, which caused him to disappear from time to time, and which had a big impact on his capacity to be creative, as you can imagine."

"Okay, so you admit you were in competition with Jay and Dylon."

"Yes, but there's nothing wrong with that. That's the nature of these competitions. I wanted to be selected for this opportunity, and so did Dylon and Jay. But at the end of the day, the best person won, and I was fine with that."

"Jay was the victim of a harassment campaign," said Odelia. "He was being sent all kinds of stuff that he didn't order, but that he was expected to pay for. And his name was being used to create online dating profiles on different websites, causing complete strangers to call him and bombard him with messages."

"And let's not forget about that burning bag of dog doo-doo," said Chase. He gave the young artist a penetrating look that made the kid wilt. "Did you have anything to do with that, Bronson?"

The kid blinked, a droplet of sweat falling from the tip of his nose. "Well... yes, I may have had something to do with some of that."

"Which part? The packages? Or the dating profiles?"

"The bag of doo-doo?" he said weakly.

"Oh, so you thought it would be a good idea to leave a burning bag on Jay's doorstep, did you?" said Chase sternly.

"Well... I thought it was a good joke, yes," the kid said, in a sort of quiet voice. He glanced down at his feet, his face flushed. "Okay, so look, I know I shouldn't have done it, but I was drunk, and upset that Jay had won the competition, so yeah, I left that bag there, and watched as he tried to put it out." His face flushed even more. "And I'm sorry, okay? It was very childish and very stupid of me."

"What about the packages? And the dating sites?"

"That wasn't me."

"Or the blackmail?" asked Odelia.

The young man looked up. "What blackmail?"

"Jay received a letter trying to blackmail him." She produced a picture of the letter on her phone.

Bronson read it and shook his head. "'I know what you did?' I don't even know what that means."

"So you didn't send this letter?"

"No, of course not. All I did was the burning bag, that's all. I didn't send any packages, or sign Jay up for any dating sites, or send him this letter. And I most definitely did not murder him or Dylon."

"Okay, Bronson, tell us where you were last night, and the night before."

Bronson claimed that he was Skyping with his mom on both nights, which was admirable, of course. And since his mom lived in Alaska, not something that was all that easy to verify. He didn't strike me as a killer, though, and he was a lousy liar, as his sweaty and flushed face could attest. Then again, he did have an excellent motive for killing both men.

The moment Bronson was back up on his scaffolding, slaving away on his big assignment, Charlene returned to have a chat with us.

"I really hope you clear up this murder business soon,"

she confessed. "We're being bombarded with complaints by angry citizens from the Cobblestone Committee. Now they're accusing the town of gross negligence, and somehow have made the assumption that we had something to do with these murders."

"How do they figure that?" asked Odelia.

"I have no idea! But since they got wind of the fact that both men were probably murdered with cobblestones, it's more grist to the mill for these people."

"Are you going to drop the cobblestone and go with asphalt?" asked Chase.

"You don't understand," said Charlene. "It was the neighborhood who asked us to redo the street with cobblestone. They wanted to create a more upscale feel, and discourage traffic from passing through their street. But once they realized that cobblestones are noisy, they changed their minds, and now a majority is against the plans. But we can't pivot like that. The budget was approved, plans were made, a contractor selected, materials bought and paid for, so abandoning the project would cost us a lot of money—would cost the community a lot of money." She sighed. "It's not always fun to be mayor, let me tell you." But then another person showed up to show their work, and we said our goodbyes.

From what I could tell, it was yet another portrait of a familiar doctor...

CHAPTER 33

"Tex is really popular, isn't he, Max?" said Dooley.

"Yes, and becoming more popular by the hour," I said.

"Three people have already entered his portrait for the art grant. So he'll probably be chosen, and then he really will be all over town."

"I very much doubt that Charlene will enter him into the competition," I said. "These art installations will represent Hampton Cove, and it probably wouldn't give a good impression if the first thing tourists see is a painting of a nude doctor."

"He's not entirely nude, though, Max. He was wearing his boxers."

"Thank God for small favors."

We were back in Uncle Alec's office, where Odelia and Chase were required to report to the Chief about any recent developments in their joint investigation.

"Okay, so at least the paper bag business has been cleared up," said the Chief, leaning back, and causing his office chair to creak under his sizable bulk. "And I've got a piece of news for you. The tech department has managed to discover the identity of the person responsible for creating those fake dating site profiles and also for the fake profiles ordering a ton of stuff online." He drummed his fingertips on his desk for effect. "And the name they came up with is Bud Zuk."

"So Jay was right," said Odelia. "The first time he and Laia came into the office he told me he thought her ex-boyfriend might be behind this, and he was."

"Which doesn't mean he's also our killer," Chase was quick to point out.

"No, but it certainly makes him a pretty good suspect in my view," said the Chief. "And one other important development: uniform talked to a witness at the scene on Tucker Street, who said she saw a woman hanging around Jay and Laia's building around the time that blackmail letter arrived." He arched his eyebrows meaningfully, and I could tell that he loved this part of his job. When the pieces of the puzzle finally started to fall into place.

"Spit it out, Chief," Chase growled, impatient.

"Laney Basula."

"Dylon's girlfriend?"

"One and the same. So I suggest," he said, leaning in and placing his beefy arms on his blotter, "that you have another little chat with both Mr. Zuk and Miss Basula. And this time make sure they tell you the truth."

༄

We met Laia's ex-boyfriend at his club, as before, though I wondered why a tennis pro who couldn't play tennis on account of his injury would still be hanging out at his club. But then I guess a tennis club is probably about more than simply playing tennis. It's also about meeting friends and influencing people.

Bud didn't seem particularly thrilled to see us, though he was gracious enough about it. No one likes to be paid a visit by the constabulary at his place of business, of course. It might set tongues wagging and before you know it you're a tennis pro no more.

"So what is it this time?" he asked, affecting a sort of faux cheerful attitude. "Another murder I didn't commit?"

But Chase decided that pictures speak louder than words, and so he placed his phone on the table in front of the young man, and showed him some evidence of the person who was behind the recent harassment campaign, IP address and all.

Chase had been right, for Bud paled beneath his tan, and when he spoke again, it was with nothing of his earlier brawn. "Okay, so yeah, I did do that," he said.

"You made fake profiles of Jay Green on several dating sites, and also several major online retailers, and then you ordered expensive items and had them shipped to Jay's address, and also connected with several women, telling them to send Jay messages on his phone and call him at all hours of the day or night. Is that what you did?"

"Yeah, that's exactly what I did," Bud confessed, without raising his eyes to meet the cop's. "When Laia broke up with me I guess I went a little crazy. So I decided to get even with the guy."

"And so you started harassing him, until finally even that wasn't enough, and you paid him a visit one night, and bashed his head in with a rock."

This time the tennis pro did look up, alarmed. "Hey, no way, man. You're not pinning that on me. Okay, so I messed with him a little, but I didn't kill the guy."

"And we're supposed to take your word for that, after you lied to us?"

"Where were you last night, Bud?" asked Odelia.

"I was right here, having dinner with members of the

board. I'm secretary of the board, you see, and..." It was as if the light suddenly came shining through. "But of course! I was here! I have witnesses. I have an alibi!" Several club members were eyeing him with unveiled curiosity, and so he quickly lowered his voice and tamped down his exuberance. "I couldn't have done it, see? I was here when it happened, wasn't I?"

"You understand we'll have to confirm your alibi?"

"Of course! Ask anyone!" Then his face fell. "Or maybe don't ask anyone. Just ask the president of the club. He's my dad. He'll confirm I was here all evening. The rest have no business with my personal business." And to emphasize his statement, he stared intently at one of the people most interested in eavesdropping on our conversation, until the person finally shrugged and looked away.

"Look, I know I've been a damn fool," said Bud, "but I love Laia. I've always loved her, and when she hooked up with Jay I was worried, really worried."

"What were you so worried about?" asked Chase.

"The guy was an artist, for crying out loud. And we all know what artists are like. Drunks, drug addicts and libertines, every last one of them. Smoking dope all night, organizing orgies, sucking down the booze by the gallon... And I didn't want that for my Laia." His face suddenly took on a sort of angelic expression, and he slowly rose to his feet. And when we looked over, we saw that none other than Laia herself was on final approach, and soon landed at our table.

"Oh, hi, Odelia," said the young woman. "Detective Kingsley. I was supposed to have lunch with Bud, but if you need him, maybe we can postpone."

"No postponing!" Bud almost yelled, but then settled down to a lower volume once more. "I think I've told you everything I know," he said, and gave Chase such a pleading look that even the hardened cop couldn't remain unaffected.

"Enjoy your lunch," he said, and got up.

"Have you found the person who killed Jay and Dylon?" asked Laia.

"The investigation is still ongoing," said Chase.

"If I were you I'd take a closer look at the person who sent us that blackmail letter," she said. "People like that can be very dangerous. I've been reading about blackmailers, and it often leads to murder."

"Thank you for the suggestion," said Chase courteously, and then we left the two young people to enjoy their lunch.

"Do you think they're a couple again, Max?" asked Dooley.

"I don't know, Dooley, but it's certainly something that Bud wants more than anything."

"Maybe now that Laia has been badly burned in love, she'll decide that Bud wasn't so bad after all," said my friend, the love expert.

CHAPTER 34

On the floor of Laney Basula's messy flat, a suitcase was lying, half-filled with items of clothing.

"Going somewhere?" asked Chase as he cut her a censorious look.

But if he thought she'd wilt under such a transparent tactic he was mistaken. Instead, she tilted her chin and said, "I've got nothing left here in this rotten town, Detective, so why not leave? Who's going to stop me? You?"

"You do realize that you're a suspect in a murder investigation," Chase pointed out. "And so I have to advise you not to leave town."

She grumbled something that didn't sound very friendly, then plunked herself down on a ratty sofa, and proceeded to freely glare at Chase. "Have you come to arrest me?"

"We've just learned that you were seen hanging around Jay Green's apartment around the time this blackmail letter was delivered." He held out his phone to show her the blackmail letter in person, but she merely shrugged.

"So?"

"So did you deliver this letter?"

She rolled her eyes. "Look, you already know I did, so just cut the theatricals, will you?"

"Why did you send this letter, Laney?" asked Odelia, adopting a more kindly tone than her detective counterpart. It's called good cop, bad cop, and Odelia excels at being the good part of this gambit.

Laney studied her fingernails, which weren't anything to write home about, I have to say. Apparently she'd done a lot of chewing on them, presumably because it's a lot cheaper than visiting a nail salon and having a pro take a whack at them.

"Me and Dylon were counting on that money," she now said. "But of course I should have expected Jay to double-cross us. That's the way he rolled."

"Jay double-crossed you?"

"Of course he did. When Dylon didn't arrive home that night, I immediately knew something was wrong. And when it turned out he didn't have the necklace on him, I knew that somehow Jay must have pulled a switcheroo of some kind. Keep the necklace and still collect that insurance money so he'd collect twice."

"But Jay wasn't home on the night your boyfriend burgled his apartment," Chase pointed out.

She shrugged. "I don't know how he did it, but somehow he did. He was devious like that, Jay was. Dylon used to tell me stories about him."

"What stories?" asked Odelia. When Laney didn't immediately respond, she added, "It's important, Laney. What stories?"

"I remember one story very distinctly. Dylon told me several times. Back when him and Jay were still in school, they used to pull pranks on the other students. You have to remember that Jay was very competitive. He always had to win, no matter what, and so once when they all had to enter an assignment for some important project, one kid came up with something brilliant. Something so amazing that he was a shoo-in for the top spot. So of course Jay couldn't have that. And so he roped Dylon into destroying that kid's assignment. Really tearing it to pieces so on the morning of the big reveal, when they pulled back the sheets from their assignments, the kid's assignment turned out to be just a pile of paper cuttings. Poor kid completely broke down. He even accused Jay and Dylon, but all they got was a slap on the wrist. I told Dylon he was a bastard for pulling such a stunt, and he agreed. Said he felt sorry for the kid, but Jay had such a hold over him that he just couldn't say no. And that's always been the dynamic between those two. Jay came up with something, and Dylon had to do his dirty work."

"Which is why you think Jay pulled a fast one on Dylon," said Odelia, nodding.

"He must have. What else could have happened to that necklace?" She idly played with the strings of her hoodie. "I guess I can tell you now. It doesn't matter now that Dylon is gone. We weren't going to deliver that necklace to Jay. Instead we were simply going to keep it and leave town. Dylon figured Jay owed him, and he thought it would net us a nice chunk of change. So when Dylon ended up dead, I just figured Jay owed me for what happened to him, which is why I ended up sending him that blackmail letter."

"Who was the kid whose assignment was destroyed?" asked Odelia.

"I don't remember. Dylon must have mentioned his name, but honestly I can't remember now."

CHAPTER 35

"I don't think Jay was a very nice person, Max," said Dooley, once we were back in the car.

"No, I don't think so either," I agreed.

"Maybe we should tell Laia. That way she won't be so sad."

"I don't know if it works like that," I said. "Even though her fiancé wasn't a nice man, that doesn't mean she will be less sad that he's dead, Dooley."

"Oh," said my friend, giving this some thought. "Yeah, I guess you're right," he said after a few moments' reflection. "If you were murdered and later on someone told me you were a bad cat, I'd still feel very sad that you were dead, Max."

"That's... very gratifying to hear, Dooley."

"It must have been Bronson," said Odelia.

"There's a very simple way to find out," said Chase, and took out his phone.

"Who are you calling?" asked Odelia, but the cop held up a finger, then spoke into his phone.

"Mr. Servais? Jake Servais? I hope I'm not interrupting

anything, sir. My name is Chase Kingsley and I'm a detective with the Hampton Cove police department. I was hoping you might remember an incident that took place several years ago. One of your students, Jay Green, pulled a prank on another student, destroying his assignment. This young man took this prank very badly. Oh, you remember it well? Would you also remember the name of the student whose work was destroyed?" He listened for a moment, then gave Odelia a knowing look, and said, "Thank you very much, sir. You've been a tremendous help." After he hung up, he said, "It was Bronson Shagreen, all right. His parents even filed a complaint with the school board, and Jay and Dylon were suspended for two weeks for the stunt."

"I think we better have another chat with Bronson," said Odelia, buckling up. "Sounds to me like he hasn't been completely honest with us."

"Poor man," said Dooley as Chase put the car in gear. "He must have been very sad when his work was destroyed."

"Yes, but was he so sad that he decided, many years later, to murder his tormentors?" I asked.

When we arrived at Town Hall, we found Bronson in the same place as before: still working hard on his new art installation, as commissioned by Charlene.

"Mr. Shagreen!" Chase called out. Not too loud, of course. We didn't want the guy to topple down from his scaffolding and break his neck.

"Oh, you're back," said Bronson. He didn't look overjoyed.

"We have some more questions for you, sir," said Chase.

"More questions?" Bronson grumbled. "It's very hard for an artist to focus on his art when people keep popping up like this," he said, but he still came crawling down to assist us in our inquiries.

"We just talked to your old school principal, Mr. Servais," said Chase.

Bronson didn't even flinch. "Yes?"

"And he told us that in your fifth year your assignment was destroyed by two of your fellow students. Jay Green and Dylon Pipe."

Bronson nodded. "That's right. Not one of my best memories."

"Perhaps you should have told us when we interviewed you earlier?"

He shrugged. "I didn't think it was relevant."

"The two men who destroyed your work were both brutally murdered, Mr. Shagreen. And you didn't think what they did to you was relevant?"

"Okay, all right. I should have told you. But you'll understand that I didn't exactly want to be reminded of such a traumatic event."

"Oh, so it was traumatic for you, was it?"

"What do you think?" the young artist said with some vehemence. "I worked hard on that assignment. Weeks of late nights. I put everything—my heart and my soul into that assignment. Only to see it completely destroyed by those two idiots."

"Your parents filed a complaint with the school board?"

"Yeah, they did. Not that it did a lot of good. They both got off with a two-week suspension, and that was it. Oh, they apologized, of course, but I could tell from their smirks that they were proud of what they did to me. And because I lost so much time, and my heart wasn't really in it the second time, my replacement assignment got a low score, which caused Jay to get the top grade that year, which of course is what it was all about in the first place."

"You still seem very bitter about the whole experience," Odelia remarked.

"Yes, of course I'm still bitter. It was a horrible thing to do."

"So when Jay and Dylon came in first and second place for this new art installation here, the decision by the town council must have rankled?"

He grimaced. "Yes, it did. And I'm not denying that. And of course Jay being Jay, he decided to rub my face in it, just for old time's sake. Sent me a message after the decision was announced, wishing me all the best, and adding that he hoped I wasn't a sore loser."

"I think we better continue this conversation at the station," said Chase.

Bronson gulped a little. "You're not... arresting me, are you?"

"I'm afraid so."

"But I told you I was Skyping with my mom when Jay and Dylon were killed."

"I talked to your mom, Bronson," said Chase, not unkindly, I thought, since he probably understood the poor kid's motive for killing his two former fellow students. "And she was honest with me. She told me she hadn't heard from you in weeks. Said you were probably too busy with your art, as usual."

"But..."

"Did you really think we wouldn't check your alibi, Bronson?"

"Or did you think your mom would lie for you?" asked Odelia.

"No, but..." The kid was sweating profusely again, clearly deeply impressed by his impending arrest. "Look, I do have an alibi, but I promised not to tell anyone."

"Of course you did," said Chase, clearly not believing a

word Bronson was saying. "Okay, let's go," he said, and took out a pair of shiny handcuffs.

I think Bronson panicked a little, for he suddenly called out, "Madam Mayor! Madam Mayor!"

Madam Mayor, who'd been talking to a council member, approached us, looking distinctly unhappy when she caught sight of Chase's handcuffs. "What's going on?" she asked.

"Bronson here is refusing to tell us where he was on the nights Jay Green and Dylon Pipe were killed," Chase explained.

"And he has a very strong motive for murdering both men," Odelia added for good measure.

"Look, he can't have killed Jay Green," said Charlene. "For the simple reason that he was with me last night."

A stunned silence followed these words, and I think we were all surprised by this development.

"Bronson was... with you?" asked Odelia.

"Poor Uncle Alec," said Dooley, voicing what I think we were all thinking. "His girlfriend is cheating on him with a promising young artist."

"I can see the attraction," I said, seeing Bronson in an entirely different light now. "Young and fit and all of that."

"If you like that sort of thing," said Dooley, a touch of disapproval in his voice.

"Yeah, exactly. If you like that sort of thing." And clearly Charlene liked it a lot, for she now stood smiling at Bronson, earning herself a frown from both Chase and Odelia. Odelia because she presumably didn't appreciate her uncle being thrown over like this, and Chase a good friend and superior officer.

When Charlene caught the expressions on their faces, she laughed. "Oh, no, it's not what you think! Bronson was modeling for us."

"Modeling?" asked Chase.

"Yeah, when Dylon died, we lost our model, and even though I like Tex a lot, he's not exactly the perfect model for these art classes we've all been taking. And so we had to find a solution, if we wanted to keep on drawing and painting. And it was actually Marge who came up with the idea. Since she didn't want to hurt her husband's feelings, she decided to organize some extra lessons. So now we have our official class, on Monday night, and a second class on Tuesday night at my place. Just a few people, mind you. Me, Marge, Vesta, Scarlett... And Bronson here, who's proven to be an excellent model and quite an inspiration for us all."

Bronson produced a faint smile. "Thanks," he murmured shyly.

"Oh, no, you've done a great job, Bronson," said Charlene, patting the young artist on the back. She then beamed at Chase. "So you see, Bronson couldn't possibly have killed Jay Green, since he was at my place last night, and there are several witnesses who can provide him with an alibi."

"Oh, dear," said Odelia.

"Now I do hope I can count on your discretion?" asked Charlene fervently. "Your dad... He's a wonderful person, but when it comes to modeling, he—"

"Sucks," said Odelia. "I get it."

"All we wanted was to prevent your dad from showing up naked again, and make an absolute fool of himself. I hope you understand."

"Yeah, of course," said Odelia, though she didn't look so understanding. I guess she didn't fully approve of her mom and grandma going behind her back like this.

"So... is Bronson our guy or not?" asked Dooley, who had a hard time following what was going on.

"No, he was privately modeling for Charlene, Marge, Gran, Scarlett and some of their friends," I explained.

"Modeling? What was he modeling?"

"Well... himself, I guess."

Dooley frowned at me. "I don't understand, Max. Why would he be modeling himself to all of these women in private?"

"It's what they do, they draw... men... in the nude."

"But why?"

"Honestly? I have absolutely no idea," I said. "For some reason they like drawing men in the nude."

"Must be something in the water," said Dooley, as he eyed the coffee cup Charlene was clutching with distinct suspicion.

CHAPTER 36

We were back in the car, with Chase prey to understandable disappointment.

"I really thought we had our guy," he said.

"Do you think I should tell Dad?" asked Odelia, who had other problems to deal with. "I mean, he has a right to know, don't you think?"

"And Uncle Alec," Dooley added. "He probably doesn't know his girlfriend spends her evenings staring at naked men."

"Bronson still doesn't have an alibi for Dylon Pipe's murder," said Chase, "but I think we can agree that Dylon and Jay were killed by the same person, so that means Bronson is off the hook. And if he didn't do it, maybe we should take a closer look at Tyrone. It's not impossible that Jay was a client of his, and in spite of his whole spiel about not wanting to hurt the people who owe him money, I'm sure he wouldn't be above putting the squeeze on them. So maybe they simply squeezed too hard and Jay ended up dead? And the same thing goes for Dylon."

"I'll talk to Mom. If anyone tells Dad it should be her," said Odelia.

"What are you talking about, babe?" asked Chase, who only now seemed to realize he was holding a monologue.

"This whole modeling business! If they don't want Dad to be their model, they should simply tell him, and not sneak behind his back like that."

"Yeah, you're absolutely right," said Chase. He put the car in gear, and moments later we happened to be cruising past Tyrone's Place. The crime boss was seated outside, enjoying a nice meal, along with several of what I assumed were his lieutenants. And as we slowly drove past, Mr. Friday had the audacity to give Chase a cheerful wave.

"The nerve of the guy!" said Chase, as he stepped on the accelerator and roared away. "Now I know it was him!"

"Yeah, but how are we going to prove it?" said Odelia.

And that's the thing, of course. When ordinary citizens commit murder, they often make a mistake, because they're amateurs, and haven't been trained for that sort of thing. But when a professional like Tyrone decides to teach a client a lesson, he doesn't make mistakes, or at least the people who work for him don't, since they're more often than not trained killers, and don't take any chances.

In other words: the investigation was more or less stymied at this point.

By the time we arrived home, Odelia had made up her mind that she was going to tell her dad that his modeling career wasn't going to pan out, with his own wife and mother-in-law deserting him for a younger model.

But when we entered the house, we found Gran and Scarlett, busily baking pancakes, with Grace the very excited recipient.

Unfortunately Grace was also a co-chef, and had been put in charge of dispensing flour to the two ladies. The upshot was that the floor was dusted in a thin layer of white, and it now looked as if it had been snowing in the kitchen.

"Gran, what are you doing!" Odelia said under her breath.

"Making pancakes, or what does it look like?" said Gran.

"Is it true that you and Mom and Charlene have been organizing a secret art class?" she asked now, the deceit obviously still rankling.

"And me," said Scarlett. "I was also there."

"I haven't forgotten about you," said Odelia, giving her grandmother's friend a frosty look.

"Honey, you have to understand we did it all for your dad," said Gran. "We didn't want to hurt his feelings by making him think we didn't like his modeling."

"But we don't like his modeling," said Scarlett.

"Yeah, I don't know what it is about your dad, but he simply doesn't inspire us to create great art, you know."

"I think it's his face," said Scarlett. "When I look at your dad I see my doctor. Probably because he is my doctor. And he reminds me of the time I had my appendix removed. I mean, who wants to think about their appendix when they're trying to create art?"

"And who wants to see their son-in-law?" Gran chimed in.

"And Bronson Shagreen inspires you, does he?" asked Odelia.

"Yes, he does, actually," said Scarlett. "Bronson *is* a work of art."

"The kid looks like a sculpture," said Gran, a blissful look appearing on her face. "He *is* a sculpture. A regular Adonis."

"I want you to come clean and tell Dad," said Odelia.

"But, honey!" Scarlett cried.

"No, it's not fair, the four of you sneaking behind his back like this."

"But he's going to ruin everything!" said Gran.

Scarlett nodded emphatically. "Yeah, this whole thing started when Tex found out that Marge was going to her art class, and that Dylon was modeling for us."

"It's all Ida's fault," said Gran. "If that woman hadn't blabbed, none of this would have happened. Tex would have been blissfully ignorant, and we would have happily been drawing away to our heart's content."

"Look, if you don't tell Dad, I will," said Odelia, really putting her foot down on this one.

"Oh, all right, but if anyone tells him, it should be Marge," said Gran. "She is, after all, his wife."

"Fine," said Odelia.

"Fine," said Gran with some vehemence. Clearly she wasn't at all happy with this state of affairs and Odelia meddling with her career as an artist. Then she gave her granddaughter a keen look. "I saw that you and Chase were talking to Charlene? Did she say anything about my contribution?"

"Or mine?" said Scarlett anxiously.

"No, she did not," said Odelia, who wasn't about to divulge classified information to these two ladies. Also, she probably had no idea who Charlene would pick.

"I wonder if they know that they both entered the exact same project," said Dooley. "And not even an actual painting but a reproduction."

"And that a lot of others probably did the same," I said.

And as Odelia continued to clear things with her nearest and dearest, Grace had fun 'helping' her great-grandmother by lightly sprinkling more flour on the floor.

And then of course the inevitable happened: the little tyke caught sight of me and Dooley, and since she felt we shouldn't be exempt from a good dusting with this fairy dust she was happily sprinkling about, she came waddling up to us, and threw a handful of the stuff on me!

"Hey, what are you doing?!" I cried. But human infants being what they are, she refused to respond, and instead dug her hand into the bag and threatened to sprinkle some more of the stuff, like a miniature fairy godmother..

And since I absolutely did not want to be turned into a snowcat, I skedaddled, chased by this ardent child, who was a lot quicker than I would have thought!

Luckily I managed to escape through the pet flap, which was too small for her. I could see her head poking through, but that was it: no matter how hard she squirmed, she couldn't follow me out. Which of course caused her to let rip a scream of frustration, followed by a bout of frantic crying. At which point her mother seemed to realize what was going on, and dragged her away from the pet flap, and I was finally at peace again.

Dooley now emerged through the flap, took one good look at me, and asked, "Max? Why are you suddenly white?"

"Because Grace covered me in flour," I explained.

"Oh, I thought you had such a shock your hair had suddenly turned white," he said, greatly relieved.

I now saw he had some flour on his own coat of fur, as well, though with him it was less noticeable, since Dooley is one of those very fluffy cats, with beigeish-grayish fur.

And as I stared at him, suddenly a thought occurred to me. It was one of those sudden flashes of inspiration that do so much to mar one's peace of mind.

"What's wrong, Max?" asked Dooley. "You look like you're suffering from an acute case of constipation."

"I need to think, Dooley," I said.

"And you also need a good wash," my friend added. "Cause that flour isn't going to wash itself off, you know."

"No, you're right," I said, but suddenly my personal hygiene was the last thing on my mind.

CHAPTER 37

Algis and Matilda Twine were watching television that night, along with their one and only daughter Laia. It was one of those family nights that neither partner had ever thought they'd share together again. But now that Laia was back home, the balance had been restored, and all was well again.

The show that was on involved famous people singing and dancing, dressed up in elaborate costumes that effectively masked their identity, with a jury that had to guess who was concealed underneath the mask.

It was all a little silly, Matilda thought, but it was still good fun, and Laia loved it, which was all that mattered.

"I'm so glad you're home again, sweetie," she said, patting her daughter's arm. "I really missed these cozy family evenings in front of the TV."

"Yeah, me too," said Laia.

"And me!" Algis piped up, as he dug into a bag of chips.

"There is one thing I wanted to ask you, though," said Laia.

"Shoot," said Matilda, who hadn't been in this good a

mood since before Laia had announced she was moving in with that loser Jay Green.

Suddenly, and to Matilda's shock, her daughter spirited a necklace from the pocket of her jeans. "Is this what I think it is?"

Matilda darted a look of annoyance at her husband. "Algis?" she said sharply.

"Yes, honey?" said Algis, not meeting her angry stare.

"What do you have to say for yourself?"

"Yes, Daddy, what do you have to say for yourself?" asked Laia, twirling the necklace around her fingers.

"Careful, sweetie," said Algis. "That thing is worth a small fortune."

"Oh, I know it is, Daddy," said Laia. "But what was it doing in your safe?"

"I... I have no idea," said Algis.

"I told you not to put it in the safe, you idiot!" Matilda couldn't help but exclaim.

"I didn't think!" said Algis.

"Okay, you need to explain something to me, cause this is all very confusing," said Laia. "This necklace was stolen from Jay's apartment by Dylon Pipe, yes?"

Matilda didn't speak, and neither did Algis.

"Before mysteriously disappearing. And now it suddenly turns up in the safe. So what does that tell us?"

"Sweetie, it's not what it looks like, " said Algis.

"Shut up, you fool," Matilda snapped.

"Let me tell you what I think happened," said Laia, idly fingering the trinket. "I think you and Dylon set up the theft of this necklace, only when Dylon fell from that window, you couldn't resist snatching that necklace from his pocket."

"That's not what happened, sweetie," said Algis.

"Shut up!" Matilda hissed.

"So how much did you promise Dylon for the safe return of my necklace?" asked Laia.

"It's not your necklace, you stupid girl!" Matilda said. "It's mine!"

"It is your mother's necklace," Algis admitted.

"So did you murder Dylon?" asked Laia. "Did you kill him so you could lay your hands on my necklace? Is that what happened?"

"Oh, sweetie," said Algis with a sigh.

"Tell me, Daddy!"

Algis reached out to his daughter, but she pulled away.

"Just tell me the truth!"

"Don't you dare," Matilda hissed.

"She has a right to know, darling," said Algis, the man with the jelly spine. "She is our daughter, and after all, we did it all for her."

"You did what for me?" Laia demanded.

"Everything," said Algis.

"Oh, God," Matilda muttered.

"Look, I'll tell you what happened, but you have to understand we only did what we thought was best for you."

"Daddy, what did you do?" asked Laia, giving him an anxious look.

"Act like an absolute fool, that's what he did," said Matilda.

"Honey..."

"This is all your fault! If you hadn't stuck your nose into that candy, we wouldn't be in this situation."

"What candy? What are you talking about?" asked Laia.

"Nose candy," said Matilda cryptically. "Your dad developed a great fondness for coke. Spent a ton of money on the evil stuff. And guess who his supplier was?"

"Dylon Pipe?"

"Bingo. Only Dylon wasn't satisfied with being paid his

regular fee. He must have discovered that Algis here is worth a great deal of money, and so he decided to supplement his income by asking a percentage on top of his usual price."

"He called it a loan," said Algis. "The little creep kept pushing me for more and more, and since I couldn't afford him blabbing to people about me being such a good customer, I had to keep paying him bigger and bigger sums of money. Until one night I simply had enough. So I decided to follow him, and demand that he give me back my money. Only he wasn't going home, but instead headed to Jay's place. I was watching from across the street, and I saw him shimmy up the drainpipe, sneak in through the window, then sneak out again, and take a nasty tumble as he did. So I looked around, crossed the street, and was planning to grab his backpack. But as I stood leaning over him, he suddenly opened his eyes and started screaming his head off, the idiot. So I panicked, grabbed the first thing I saw, and hit him on the head to shut him up. Only I must have hit him too hard."

"And killed the kid in the process," Matilda muttered. She was still angry when she thought about it. Her husband arriving home that night with this kid's backpack, which contained her necklace, and confessing that he'd killed some lowlife drug dealer. At least he'd had the good sense to dump the stone into the canal, and make sure he wasn't seen.

"So you killed Dylon?" asked Laia, aghast.

"It was an accident!" Algis cried.

"It doesn't sound like an accident to me," said Laia.

"The kid had been pestering me, blackmailing me. I was at the end of my rope."

"And high as a kite," Matilda added.

"I've already told you, I'm going to quit, honey," said Algis.

"Don't you honey me!" said Matilda.

"Okay, so what about Jay?" asked Laia.

Matilda closed her mouth with a click, and Algis looked away.

"Oh, my God, you killed him, too, didn't you!"

"Yeah, well, the kid was going to destroy your future," said Matilda finally.

A look of horror now appeared on Laia's face. "Mommy!"

Matilda sighed. "Like your dad said, it was for your own good, sweetie. That man was going to ruin your life. So it's all for the best. Now can we watch the show? I actually think Steve Harvey is underneath that mask."

"What... when... How could you!"

"Look, I agree with your mother," said Algis. "I did what I had to do, and I'm not sorry." He gave his daughter a sweet smile. "One day, when you have kids of your own, you will understand."

"Tell me exactly what happened," said Laia, suddenly adopting a steely tone.

Matilda sighed, then nodded to her husband. "Better tell her."

"I found Dylon's phone in his backpack, which is how I knew that he and Jay had worked this thing together. Stealing the necklace as an insurance scam. Which is when I decided to pay that young man a visit. I knew you were out with your friends, and so I dropped by the apartment to give him a piece of my mind. Tell him to stay away from you, you know. Only when I got there, he just laughed in my face. Called me an old so-and-so, and became belligerent. So I..." He licked his lips, and glanced at Matilda. "I hit him. I didn't mean to hit very hard, but I guess I don't know my own strength."

"And once again, you were high as a kite," said Matilda dryly.

"One line for courage, darling. Just the one line."

"Daddy, the police told me Jay's face was flat as a pancake.

That he'd sustained so many blows there was nothing left. So don't tell me you just hit him once."

"It was a very heavy rock," said Algis feebly.

"You took a rock in there? So you intended to kill him?"

"No! I just took it as insurance. You know, just in case."

Laia turned to her mom. "Did you know about this?"

"Know about it? I told him to go there!" Matilda said. "It was my idea!"

"He was a very bad man, sweetie," said Algis, trying to take his daughter into an embrace. A foolish thing to do, of course, for Laia blew up.

"You're crazy! You're both crazy! Who are you people! I don't even know you!"

"We're your parents," said Matilda. "And we would do anything for you."

Suddenly Matilda's eye was drawn to a wire peeking out from her daughter's blouse. And as she grabbed it and pulled, an entire device popped out.

"What's this?" she demanded. "Are you recording us, you stupid girl!"

"Yes, Mommy," said Laia. "And for your information, the police have heard everything you just said." She got up with as much dignity as she could muster, and stared down at her parents, who were both immobile with shock. "And for your information: I loved Jay and he loved me. And I'll never forgive you!"

And in just that moment, a small contingent of cops stormed into the room, and before Matilda knew what was happening, she was being placed under arrest, and so was Algis.

CHAPTER 38

"Okay, so how did you do it, Max?" asked Brutus. "How did you find out it was Laia's parents?"

We were in the backyard, the four of us seated on the porch swing, while the humans were all gathered around the garden table, enjoying a small feast. Food should have been provided by Tex, our go-to grill master. Only Tex had announced he was on strike. Marge and Gran had told him about their secret art class, and Tex had taken the betrayal hard. And so now he was on strike, both as a model, even though his services weren't really required, and as a dispenser of food.

Though judging from the happy faces all around, no one seemed to mind particularly that the good doctor had downed tools.

Instead, Chase had taken over, and with the assistance of Uncle Alec had done a wonderful job. They'd even earned themselves applause from their family, something I don't think Tex had ever received.

It only served to make the paterfamilias even more cranky, and for a while it had looked as if he would also refuse to take nourishment, but in the end I guess even he realized that was overdoing things. Though it may have been the delicious smells wafting from the grill that finally decided him.

I watched Grace smear her face with what looked like some kind of vegetable paste and said, with a smile, "It was actually Grace who solved the case."

"Grace!" Harriet cried, eyeing the toddler with newfound respect. "She's not even old enough to speak and already she's solving cases!"

"Well, she didn't actually solve the case, but she did give me a very important clue," I clarified, lest there be any misunderstanding. "Flour."

"Flour?"

"Flour. You see, the day we paid a visit to the Twines, Algis was baking pancakes, and his shirtfront was covered with flour. Only he also had some flour under his nose, which Matilda hastened to wipe off. Now how would a man get flour up the nose?"

"Unless it wasn't flour but something else entirely," said Harriet, understanding dawning.

"What was it, Max?" asked Dooley. "Was it sugar?"

"Not sugar, Dooley, but cocaine. Algis Twine is an addict, and Dylon Pipe was his dealer. Only Dylon kept 'borrowing' more and more money from the man, implying that if he didn't pay up, he would reveal his dirty secret, so finally Algis was fed up, and after another one of their late-night meetings, where money and drugs changed hands, he decided to follow Dylon, who was on his way to break into Jay's place and steal that necklace. And that's how Algis found out what was going on."

"And bashed in his dealer's head," said Harriet, nodding. "And it was the flour that did it, was it?"

"Well, Gran was baking pancakes, and Grace happened to

cover me in the stuff, which is how I suddenly remembered our interview with Laia's parents, which made me wonder if Algis hadn't told us the whole truth. That, and the fact that he used to be a bruiser for an extremist organization back in the day when he was young and poor. His nickname was The Bludgeoner, and he loved smashing people's heads in. So I guess that experience served him well when dealing with Dylon and Jay."

"But why did he kill Jay?" asked Brutus.

"Because he wanted to save his daughter from an unhappy marriage. He figured that if Jay and Dylon were such great friends, Jay was just as bad as Dylon, and would lead his little girl to her ruin. And he couldn't have that."

"He could have argued with the guy. Or offered him money to walk away."

"Which is exactly what he did, but then Jay must have figured he was coming into plenty of money from his insurance scam, and he was still hoping that necklace would turn up, so he could sell it for a nice chunk of change."

"Algis must have been pretty enraged to kill the guy in such a brutal way," said Harriet.

"Yeah, well, I guess his Bludgeoner days suddenly made a comeback. And also, he was high on the white powder at the time, courtesy of Dylon Pipe's provisions."

"So a dusting of flour and you caught a killer," said Brutus, giving me a nod of approval. "Well done, Max."

"There was also the fact that the killer had felt Laia's pulse. What killer would do such a thing? It was one of those little things that kept nagging me throughout the investigation. And then it hit me: a father would want to make sure his daughter was all right. Which is also where that second phone call came from. Just before the neighbor called the police, Algis had already called 911, making sure Laia would get the proper treatment, and not lie there for hours until someone happened to stumble across her."

Odelia now walked over, laden with delicious treats. We welcomed her with open paws, so to speak.

"Is Tex ever going to speak to Marge again?" asked Dooley anxiously. "I don't like it when they are fighting, Odelia."

"Oh, I'm sure everything will work out," said Odelia with a wink. "In fact Mom has already promised not to draw naked men anymore. Instead, they're going to paint cats from now on."

"Cats!" Harriet cried. "Not... stuffed cats!"

"No, live ones," said Odelia. "And more specifically, they're going to paint you guys."

"But I don't want to be painted," Brutus lamented. "Paint is bad for the skin, and it's toxic when ingested."

"They're not going to actually paint you, Brutus," said Odelia. "They're going to create a painting *of* you."

"Oh," said Brutus. "Well, I guess that's all right, then."

"Of course it's all right. And this time my dad is even going to join in the fun. And all you have to do is sit still for a couple of hours and pose."

We all gulped. "Sit still for a couple of hours?" I asked weakly. "But how?"

"I can't sit still for hours," said Harriet. "I have to go for a tinkle, have a bite to eat..." She shook her head decidedly. "I'm sorry, Odelia. But no can do. You'll just have to find yourself a different cat model. Or better yet, a stuffed one."

Odelia thought for a moment, then said, "Or you could simply take a long nap while we paint you."

"Now you're talking," I said.

"Don't say yes, Max," said Harriet. "It's probably a trick. I mean, what's so interesting about a sleeping cat?"

"You'd be surprised," said Odelia. "Watching a cat sleep is very soothing, and soothing is all the rage right now."

She was right. After Tex's whole semi-nude posing business, we all needed something soothing. Tex had proved a big hit at Charlene's upcoming art show, but in the end the town council had decided to go in a different direction. I guess they didn't want to scare off the tourists. So now the theme was pets. And you have to admit: who doesn't like a pet? And so many possibilities offered themselves: some people keep pet turtles, others keep pet rabbits, chickens, hamsters, parrots... Though of course the absolute king of pets is still Felis catus.

"Here," said Odelia, taking out her phone. "We've already started making some preliminary sketches. I've done Max." A very smart-looking blorange specimen appeared, and I nodded approvingly. "Mom did Dooley." A nice gray fluffball, nicely rendered. "Chase did Brutus."

"Very nice," Brutus murmured.

He looked like a cross between Rambo and Terminator, only the feline version.

"And finally Gran did Harriet."

A sort of ratty growth appeared on her phone's screen. We all recoiled in horror.

"But... I look like the stuff you fish out of the shower drain!" Harriet cried.

"Are you showing them my drawing, Odelia?" asked Gran happily. "What do you think? Pretty hot stuff, huh?"

But Harriet didn't approve. Instead, she drew herself up to her full height, and cried, "I've had it with you people! First you kidnap me, then you put me to work as an art slave, then you cover me in toxic paint and threaten to stuff me, and now you turn me into this disgusting shower hairball! Well, you can all get stuffed!"

And with these immortal words, she stalked off, head high, tail even higher.

Gran watched her leave, and shrugged. "Oh, well. I guess everyone's a critic."

THE END

Thanks for reading! If you want to know when a new Nic Saint book comes out, sign up for Nic's mailing list: nicsaint.com/news

EXCERPT FROM PURRFECT SLUG (MAX 53)

Chapter One

As it happens, a dark cloud had descended upon my hometown. And to think that the day had started out so sunny and bright. But then of course I'm not a fortune teller, so it's always hard for me to know what is going to take place in the near or distant future. All I know is that I woke up experiencing a certain malaise, which is not my custom. And then of course Grace, our human's little girl, discovered that cats have tails, and decided that pulling those tails provides a limitless source of joy, and so she'd been chasing my tail for the best part of the morning. Each time I thought I was safe, and had shaken off the infernal infant, there she was, giggling and gibbering, as human infants are in the habit of doing, and making a dive for my tail, giving it a forceful yank the moment she managed to take hold of the sensitive appendage. Not a pleasant way to pass the morning!

"Why does she keep doing this!" Dooley cried, since he, too, had become a victim of Grace's latest game. So much so that we'd taken cover in the backyard, hiding behind the rose bushes, where Grace had yet to root us out.

"She seems to derive a certain pleasure from the process," I said as I nervously scanned the horizon, just in case our newfound nemesis staged a comeback.

"But why? What's so funny about pulling a cat's tail?"

"I'm not sure," I said, "but it seems there is something inherently fascinating about a tail that appeals to the youthful zeal these infants possess in spades."

It was one more aspect of cohabiting with a human infant that we hadn't taken into account on that fateful day when Odelia had announced that soon two would become three, and that our home was to be blessed with Kingsley offspring.

So far I hadn't experienced much of the joy a baby is supposed to bring. If Grace wasn't pulling our tails, she was vomiting all over our precious fur, or digging a chubby little hand into our food bowls and spreading kibble across the kitchen floor, like a farmer sowing seeds. Or dunking certain objects into our drinking bowls, such as there are: a rubber ball, a pacifier, or a stuffed elephant.

"Oh, where are the days when it was just us and Odelia," I said with a deep sigh, as I placed my head on my front paws, without relaxing my vigilance, lest our formidable foe suddenly appeared out of the blue, as she often does.

"It's all Chase's fault," said Dooley. "If Odelia hadn't met him, she wouldn't have married him, and if she hadn't married him, Grace wouldn't have shown up."

And as we both moodily stared before ourselves, silently blaming Chase Kingsley for this horrible predicament we found ourselves in, a tiny voice suddenly sounded in my ears. It wasn't Grace, that much was obvious, for she might be a baby, but she has a voice like an opera singer when she's going well.

No, this voice was so weak it could have been my tummy

rumbling and expressing its distress at having to drink water laced with stuffed elephant residue, or eating kibble that has been used to sweep the kitchen floor.

"Help me!" the tiny voice called out.

I glanced over to my friend. But Dooley's lips weren't moving, and unless he'd suddenly turned into a ventriloquist, it was clear it wasn't him asking for help.

"Can you please help me!" the voice repeated, a little louder this time, and more emphatically.

So I glanced around in all directions, my head turning this way and that, and that's when I finally saw it: a snail was sneaking along the branches of the rose bush we were currently using as cover. The snail was staring at me with helpless bewilderment, and repeated, "Help me, please! I'm hanging on for dear life here!"

As far as I could tell, the snail was firmly glued to that branch, as snails do, and wasn't in any immediate danger. Still, obviously she or he—or it—was going through a personal crisis of some kind, for its feelers waved back and forth, as if trying to draw my attention, and then it said, "It-it's going to eat me!"

"What's going to eat you?" I asked, curious about this creature's distress.

"What's going to eat what?" asked Dooley, who'd opened his eyes to take in the strange scene. "Oh, hey there, little guy. How are you doing?"

"Not well, cat," said the snail. "If I'm not careful, that big bird is going to eat me with hide and hair!"

"I didn't know snails had hair," said Dooley, interested. "Though I can understand how being eaten is not a fun prospect. I wouldn't like it myself."

"Please chase it away," said the snail. "I know birds don't like cats, and so if you could please do me this one little favor, I'll make it worth your while."

EXCERPT FROM PURRFECT SLUG (MAX 53)

I looked around for a sign of this bird the snail was talking about, and lo and behold: there was indeed a bird, perched on the top branch of the rose bush, eyeing our slimy little friend with distinct relish reflected in its beady eyes.

"Now shoo, bird," I said sternly, and waved an admonishing paw in the direction of the bird. "Take a hike, will you? Nothing to see here so move along."

The bird shifted its gaze from the snail to me, and didn't seem to like what it saw, for it frowned darkly. "If you know what's good for you, you won't come between me and my meal, cat," said the bird with a sort of menacing undertone.

"And what if I do?" I said, not liking the attitude of this bird one little bit.

I'd raised myself up to my full height, which, I have to say, is considerable, and to my satisfaction I saw how the bird seemed to flinch a bit when it saw what it was up against. So finally the bird—it could have been a sparrow, or it could have been a robin, my knowledge of the different bird species is shamefully limited— growled, "Oh, all right. Have it your way." And after directing one final longing look at our new friend the snail, it spread its wings and flew off, to live and catch another snail another day, I guess.

"Phew, tanks, cat," said the snail, as it visibly relaxed now that the danger had passed. "That bird had been following me around for quite a while now!"

"I don't understand why birds eat snails anyway," said Dooley. "Isn't it difficult to digest, with all of that slime? And not very tasty either, I would imagine."

"And let's not forget about the shell," I said. I couldn't imagine trying to swallow down a whole shell. I'm sure it would feel like a brick in my stomach. Then again, birds are strange creatures. And probably possess concrete stomachs.

I'd already taken my position underneath that bush again, preparatory to taking a light nap, when the snail said, "I said

EXCERPT FROM PURRFECT SLUG (MAX 53)

I'd make it worth your while, and my name wouldn't be Rupert if I didn't keep my promise. So here goes, cats."

"Here goes what?" asked Dooley, glancing around to see what other slimy creatures would come crawling out from the undergrowth.

"It's an expression, Dooley," I said as I stifled a yawn. "It means he's going to do something."

"Do what?"

"I don't know. Something." Frankly I was feeling a little sleepy right around then. I guess it was because of the adrenaline dissipating from my system. That and being chased around the house by Grace had sapped my strength. So whatever wisdom the snail was intent on imparting, I scarcely paid attention, and even as I dozed off, I was conscious of strange words being spoken by the snail.

"Blue moon," he said. Or words to that effect.

If only I'd paid closer attention, and hadn't allowed my natural vigilance to waver at that crucial moment, it might have saved me a whole lot of trouble!

Chapter Two

Tex had been pottering around in his backyard, weeding the flowerbeds and thinking up ways and means of beautifying his modest little patch of paradise, when his thoughts of floral delight were rudely interrupted by his neighbor Ted, who desired speech.

"Say, Tex," said Ted, his head popping up over the hedge that served as a natural barrier between both gardens. "I've been thinking."

"Well, that's a first," Tex muttered under his breath, as he reluctantly downed tools. It wasn't that he disliked his neighbor, but it couldn't be said he liked him a great deal either. There had always existed a certain rivalry between both men,

EXCERPT FROM PURRFECT SLUG (MAX 53)

especially when it came to the fate of their respective backyards. Tex had long been a big proponent of the common garden gnome as a way of lending that little *je-ne-sais-quoi* to his property, and Ted had more or less brazenly copied the idea. The result was a sort of garden gnome race between the two homeowners.

"I've been thinking we should pool our resources and hire a professional landscaper," said Ted, as he rubbed his nose then sneezed.

Tex frowned at his neighbor. "What are you talking about? What landscaper?"

He'd gotten up from his position on the foam pad he used to protect his knees and approached the hedge. At one point they'd agreed to a fence to mark the official boundary, but recently had decided that a hedge was much nicer, and also provided a way for their respective pets to come and go as they pleased. Ted and his wife Marcie owned a sheepdog, Rufus, who, contrary to popular belief, wasn't an enemy to the Poole cat contingent but a friend, and so as Ted and Tex chatted across the hedge, Tex saw that Harriet and Brutus scooted underneath, and crossed into Ted's backyard to shoot the breeze with the man's canine friend.

"Look, I know you take great pride in your backyard, Tex," said Ted. "And you know I do, too. But at the end of the day, we're hardly pros, are we? And you have to admit it takes a lot of time and effort to make these gardens shine. So I was thinking that maybe if we bring in a landscaper, and then pay a gardener to come in once a week, or once every two weeks, we could save ourselves a lot of trouble, and at the same time have the kind of backyards we can really be proud of."

"Mh," said Tex as he gave this suggestion some thought. The idea had merit. Though he was reluctant to admit it to his neighbor, of course. So instead he said, "Professional

EXCERPT FROM PURRFECT SLUG (MAX 53)

landscapers are expensive, Ted. Even if we pooled our resources."

"Oh, I'm sure between the two of us, it's a warranted expenditure," said Ted. With a wink, he added, "I might even be able to turn it into a tax deduction."

Ted was an accountant, so creating tax breaks or write-offs was what he did.

"I'd have to discuss it with Marge," said Tex, wavering. He enjoyed working in his backyard, but lately he'd started feeling the strain, especially when spring was in the land, of spending every available moment having to fight the good fight against the pesky weeds attacking his flowerbeds. Even the modest patch of lettuce and radish he'd planted at Marge's instigation needed constant vigilance to save them from a veritable army of pests trying to get at them before Tex could.

"Look, I know you need some time to think about it," said Ted, "but give it some serious thought, yeah? I think you'll find it will make both our lives a lot easier. And hey, paying a gardener doesn't mean we can't still do a little bit of gardening ourselves. Only difference is that we'll have fun doing it, and not see it as a chore we can't get out of." He shrugged. "At least that's how I feel. You?"

Tex slowly nodded. "Lately it's all becoming a little too much," he admitted. "Especially those snails that keep eating everything I plant."

"Yeah, same here," said Ted. "And you should see what they're doing to my gnomes. Every morning those little buddies are full of slimy trails. Really yucky."

It was a problem the good doctor had been contending with himself, and he could sympathize.

"I just hope this landscaper of yours goes easy on the toxic products."

"Oh, no! Natural stuff only," Ted assured him. "Absolutely.

EXCERPT FROM PURRFECT SLUG (MAX 53)

We don't want to poison the soil, now do we?" And with a final nod at his neighbor, Ted returned to the arduous work of having to clean his gnomes from all traces of snail slime.

It was an arduous task, and a thankless one at that. For no sooner had they cleaned their respective gnomes, an army of snails had defaced them again.

And so it was with a faint sense of hope that Tex returned to his weeding. For once in his life, Ted had had a good idea. An idea Tex could wholeheartedly get behind. And if this gardener proved a tax break, so much the better. Your hard-working doctor has to count the pennies, just like any responsible family man.

Chapter Three

While Tex stood chatting with his neighbor, Harriet and Brutus had slipped through the hedge and were now engaged in earnest conversation with Rufus, the Trappers' sheepdog. As a rule, cats and dogs don't usually see eye to eye, but then life in Hampton Cove doesn't always adhere to the fixed rules that seem to govern the rest of the world.

"I don't think so, Rufus," Harriet was saying. "I really believe you should go through with it."

"But Harriet," Rufus said, directing a look of anguish at his neighbor. "How can you be so sure?"

"Because you are just about the handsomest dog I know, that's why," said Harriet. A rare compliment in her book, but one that was well deserved, she felt.

"I don't know," said the big fluffy dog, as he hung his head, prey to indecision. "What if I lose badly? I'll never live it down. You know what pets are like."

Oh, she most certainly did. Once she had given her all by launching herself into show business, only to be laughed off the stage by a roomful of haters. So she could see where

Rufus was coming from. Which is why she felt so adamant about this. "Look, Rufus," she said, deciding to go for broke. "If you do this, I'll be there for you every step of the way. And I'm talking personal one-on-one coaching. I'll be your personal trainer, mental coach and psychologist all rolled into one."

"And me," said Brutus, a little gruffly, Harriet felt. "Don't forget about me."

"You would do that for me?" asked Rufus, a smile breaking through the clouds.

"Of course!" said Harriet. "And if you make it, which I'm sure you will, it will be because we gave it everything we had. It will be a celebration of the art of perseverance." And her personal vengeance against all the naysayers that claimed she was a talentless hack. Of which, she had to say, there were plenty.

"What about you, Brutus?" asked Rufus, consulting Harriet's mate. "Do you think I should sign myself up for this dog show or not?"

Brutus hesitated for a moment, but then caught Harriet's eye. "Of course," said the butch black cat. "I think you're a very talented dog, Rufus, and it's about time the world saw you for who you are."

Rufus beamed widely. If even Brutus felt that their friend had a chance, he might as well go ahead. "Could you give Fifi the same speech you just gave me?"

"Fifi?" asked Harriet. "Does she also want to join the show?"

"Oh, absolutely," said Rufus. "In fact it was her idea. Only she doesn't feel she's pretty enough to enter such an important competition, so she bailed."

"I think Fifi stands just as much chance as you," said Harriet, and hoped her words rang true with the power of conviction. She'd never understood why dogs enter these

EXCERPT FROM PURRFECT SLUG (MAX 53)

Best in Show deals, but then she'd always relied more on her innate sense of talent rather than her good looks. But it was certainly true that both Rufus and Fifi were prime specimens of their respective species, and would have no trouble finding plenty of supporters to defend their claim at the big prize.

"Okay, if I've got you both in my corner, I think I might give this thing a shot," finally Rufus decided. He heaved a deep sigh. "Now all we need to do is to convince Ted and Marcie to enter me into the competition. And Kurt, of course."

They exchanged worried glances. Convincing Ted and Marcie was one thing, but Fifi's human was quite another. A retired schoolteacher, the notoriously bad-tempered Kurt Mayfield wasn't the kind of person to take advice from his neighbors, and the only way to enter both dogs in the competition was for Harriet to tell Gran or Marge, and for Gran or Marge to talk to their neighbors and float the idea. If either Rufus or Fifi's humans decided against the idea, no dice!

"Oh, it will be fine," said Harriet, as she gently patted the big dog on in the flank. "Kurt will have to agree. He just has to."

"If Fifi doesn't sign up, neither will I," said Rufus, in a strong example of canine loyalty.

"Fifi will sign up. And if Kurt refuses," said Harriet, "we'll sign her up in secret. He'll never even know she entered the show until it's all over and done with."

"Yeah, but someone has to walk her onto the platform," said Rufus. "And if not Kurt, then who?"

Harriet smiled a fine smile. "Just leave that to me," she said, as an idea was already starting to form in her resourceful mind.

ABOUT NIC

Nic has a background in political science and before being struck by the writing bug worked odd jobs around the world (including but not limited to massage therapist in Mexico, gardener in Italy, restaurant manager in India, and Berlitz teacher in Belgium).

When he's not writing he enjoys curling up with a good (comic) book, watching British crime dramas, French comedies or Nancy Meyers movies, sampling pastry (apple cake!), pasta and chocolate (preferably the dark variety), twisting himself into a pretzel doing morning yoga, going for a run, and spoiling his big red tomcat Tommy.

He lives with his wife (and aforementioned cat) in a small village smack dab in the middle of absolutely nowhere and is probably writing his next 'Mysteries of Max' book right now.

www.nicsaint.com

ABOUT NIC

Nic has a background in political science and, before being struck by the writing bug, worked odd jobs around the world (including, but not limited to, massage therapist in Mexico, goatherder in Italy, restaurant manager in India, and PA for a teacher in Belarus).

When he's not writing he enjoys curling up with a good (comic) book, watching British crime dramas, French comedies or Nancy Meyers movies, sampling pastry (apple strudel, pasta and chocolate (preferably the dark variety), twisting himself into a pretzel doing morning yoga, going for a run and spoiling his big, red tomcat Thump.

He lives with his wife and aforementioned cat in a small village smack dab in the middle of absolutely nowhere and is probably writing his next Adventures of Max books right now.

www.nicestaller.com

ALSO BY NIC SAINT

The Mysteries of Max
Purrfect Murder
Purrfectly Deadly
Purrfect Revenge
Purrfect Heat
Purrfect Crime
Purrfect Rivalry
Purrfect Peril
Purrfect Secret
Purrfect Alibi
Purrfect Obsession
Purrfect Betrayal
Purrfectly Clueless
Purrfectly Royal
Purrfect Cut
Purrfect Trap
Purrfectly Hidden
Purrfect Kill
Purrfect Boy Toy
Purrfectly Dogged
Purrfectly Dead
Purrfect Saint
Purrfect Advice
Purrfect Passion

A Purrfect Gnomeful
Purrfect Cover
Purrfect Patsy
Purrfect Son
Purrfect Fool
Purrfect Fitness
Purrfect Setup
Purrfect Sidekick
Purrfect Deceit
Purrfect Ruse
Purrfect Swing
Purrfect Cruise
Purrfect Harmony
Purrfect Sparkle
Purrfect Cure
Purrfect Cheat
Purrfect Catch
Purrfect Design
Purrfect Life
Purrfect Thief
Purrfect Crust
Purrfect Bachelor
Purrfect Double
Purrfect Date
Purrfect Hit
Purrfect Baby
Purrfect Mess
Purrfect Paris

Purrfect Model

The Mysteries of Max Box Sets

Box Set 1 (Books 1-3)
Box Set 2 (Books 4-6)
Box Set 3 (Books 7-9)
Box Set 4 (Books 10-12)
Box Set 5 (Books 13-15)
Box Set 6 (Books 16-18)
Box Set 7 (Books 19-21)
Box Set 8 (Books 22-24)
Box Set 9 (Books 25-27)
Box Set 10 (Books 28-30)
Box Set 11 (Books 31-33)
Box Set 12 (Books 34-36)
Box Set 13 (Books 37-39)
Box Set 14 (Books 40-42)
Box Set 15 (Books 43-45)
Box Set 16 (Books 46-48)

The Mysteries of Max Big Box Sets

Big Box Set 1 (Books 1-10)
Big Box Set 2 (Books 11-20)

The Mysteries of Max Shorts

Purrfect Santa (3 shorts in one)
Purrfectly Flealess
Purrfect Wedding
Purrfect Fuzz
Purrfect Love

Nora Steel
Murder Retreat

The Kellys
Murder Motel
Death in Suburbia

Emily Stone
Murder at the Art Class

Washington & Jefferson
First Shot

Alice Whitehouse
Spooky Times
Spooky Trills
Spooky End
Spooky Spells

Ghosts of London
Between a Ghost and a Spooky Place
Public Ghost Number One
Ghost Save the Queen
Box Set 1 (Books 1-3)
A Tale of Two Harrys
Ghost of Girlband Past
Ghostlier Things

Charleneland
Deadly Ride
Final Ride

Neighborhood Witch Committee

Witchy Start

Witchy Worries

Witchy Wishes

Saffron Diffley

Crime and Retribution

Vice and Verdict

Felonies and Penalties (Saffron Diffley Short 1)

The B-Team

Once Upon a Spy

Tate-à-Tate

Enemy of the Tates

Ghosts vs. Spies

The Ghost Who Came in from the Cold

Witchy Fingers

Witchy Trouble

Witchy Hexations

Witchy Possessions

Witchy Riches

Box Set 1 (Books 1-4)

The Mysteries of Bell & Whitehouse

One Spoonful of Trouble

Two Scoops of Murder

Three Shots of Disaster

Box Set 1 (Books 1-3)

A Twist of Wraith

A Touch of Ghost

A Clash of Spooks

Box Set 2 (Books 4-6)

The Stuffing of Nightmares

A Breath of Dead Air

An Act of Hodd

Box Set 3 (Books 7-9)

A Game of Dons

Standalone Novels

When in Bruges

The Whiskered Spy

ThrillFix

Homejacking

The Eighth Billionaire

The Wrong Woman

CPSIA information can be obtained
at www.ICGtesting.com
Printed in the USA
BVHW030733170423
662367BV00013B/1347